Dedication

To my husband JD: thank you for being patient with me while writing this, and for being my own personal Nicolai. To my children Lucas, Lily, Lylah, & Kirra: you are the reason I write, live, and love. Without any of you, this second book would not have been possible.

Crimson Moon

The Crimson Chronicles Series
Book 2

By
Christine Gabriel

pandamoon
publishing

www.pandamoonpublishing.com

Jacket design and illustrations © Pandamoon Publishing
Art Direction by Don Kramer: Pandamoon Publishing
Editing by Zara Kramer, Rachel Schoenbauer, Forrest Driskel, and Heather Stewart: Pandamoon Publishing

Pandamoon Publishing and the portrayal of a panda and a moon are registered trademarks of Pandamoon Publishing.

Library of Congress Cataloging-in-Publication Data is on file at the Library of Congress, Washington, DC

Edition: 1, version 1.01 2019
ISBN 13: 978-1-945502-54-5

Crimson Moon

Chapter 1
Premonition

The mist covered the ground like the white veil over a new bride's face. The air was thick with smoke, smelling of death and decay. The birds were no longer singing their sweet songs, nor were there any immediate signs of life in the area. The charred ground crunched under my feet and I realized it was the only sound I could hear in the eerie silence. I looked up at the once milky moon and cringed at its new bright crimson color. *What could've possibly caused the moon to turn blood red?*

When I had left, it had been fall and the trees that had once been graced by beautiful leaves were now dark and barren. It was apparent that something terrible had happened to the world I had fought so hard to protect and it was imperative I found the cause of it quickly.

"Don't move!" a voice commanded from behind me.

My body stiffened and a strong tingling sensation began to course through my fingertips. This person obviously had no clue who they were dealing with.

"I said, 'Don't move.'"

"Am I allowed to breathe?" I retorted sarcastically.

"Who are you, and what are you doing in this part of the woods?"

"You know, I was once asked a question very similar to that one."

"I don't have time for your sarcastic remarks. The dark one could be watching."

"Why do all bad guys have such dumb nicknames?"

"Don't act foolish. You know exactly who he is."

"Well, apparently you've been misinformed because I have absolutely no idea who you're referring to."

The charred earth popped and cracked under the heavy footsteps of the person behind me. The familiar rush of adrenaline pumped through my veins, and my fists clenched in silent anticipation of the situation at hand. Something sharp and cold pressed into the small of my back.

"You don't want to do that," I hissed through clenched teeth.

"Are you threatening me?"

Spinning around, I faced my attacker. "No, in fact, I think it's you who are threatening me." The surprise on my face matched his once we realized who we were each talking to.

Shocked by this discovery, I blinked and cleared my throat. "Mathias, what are you doing here?"

"I guess I could ask you the same question," he replied, still wielding the spear-like weapon defensively in front of my face.

"Mathias, put the weapon down," I coaxed gently. "I don't want to have to hurt you."

He looked around nervously before lowering his weapon. "I'm sorry, Angelina. I didn't expect to see you here." He leaned in closer and whispered, "If he finds you, he'll kill you."

I stared into his dull gray eyes and wondered where their ever-changing color had gone. "Who will kill me?"

He stared at me in surprise. "You really don't know."

I shook my head. "No, I don't."

He glanced nervously over his shoulder, almost expecting some unseen enemy to jump out from behind one of the charred trees and attack him. "Hurry, come with me." He motioned for me to follow him. "If he knew I was helping you, he would end my life for sure."

The fear in Mathias' eyes and the way he was acting frightened me. He had always been so confident and strong. Hopefully, I could get some answers out of him and find out what was going on.

Chapter 2
Ruins

I followed him through the barren forest and noticed we were heading toward a familiar place. Anxiety settled into the back of my mind, and I rubbed at the soft prickle of arm hair that had begun to push slightly against the inside of my sweatshirt. We were deep in the forest now, and the odd rock formations that hid Nicolai's family lay ahead.

My mouth dropped open. The once beautiful rune-covered rocks had been toppled over and crushed. My heart sunk once I saw the gaping hole in the middle of the debris. Someone or something had infiltrated their sacred home.

He led me down the stairs and into the darkness. "Watch your step."

I nodded and put my hand against the cool wall to help guide my way down the steep steps. The light from the gaping hole illuminated our way through the darkness. We rounded the hallway and the once beautiful door that held itself between their world and ours was no longer standing. The walls were covered in blackened grime and charred, wood chunks were scattered around our feet. The smell of smoke hung heavy in the air.

"Explosives," Mathias said without hesitation.

Guilt and sadness filled my heart. Why did I suddenly have the overwhelming feeling that I was to blame for this?

"Be careful," Mathias warned as he cautiously made his way through the blackened doorway.

"Why?" I asked, immediately answering my own question as I sidestepped the numerous traps that were spread across the ground. I looked up at the dark ceiling and my heart sank. The diamonds that had graced the ceiling of this wondrous place and had filled it with its intriguing glow were gone. The once extravagant buildings were unrecognizable with most of them caving in on themselves. Everything had been destroyed. All of it…gone.

"This way." Mathias pointed towards Ctephanyi's house, which was surprisingly unscathed.

"It's not damaged?"

"No." He shook his head. "Ctephanyi used the blood of their ancestors to create a magic field that no mortal or immortal could cross or destroy." He put his hand up against the invisible force field and motioned for me to walk through.

"But you just said we couldn't cross through it."

He smiled. "She made it safe for us to walk through."

"You're sure?"

"You question Ctephanyi's use of magic?"

My eyes narrowed in hesitation. "I question a lot of things in regard to Ctephanyi."

"And understandably so, but you trust me, right?"

Hesitating for another moment, I finally let out a long sigh and nodded. "I trust you."

I lifted my hand slowly and lay it next to his. A low, electric current ran through my body. I yanked my hand away in surprise and he laughed again. "See?"

Amazed, I touched it again. "It really doesn't hurt."

"Don't let it fool you. This magic field would incinerate anyone other than those protected."

My eyes widened at the thought. "Well, that's kind of scary."

"Well, look at who created it," he said.

"Yeah, you've got a point there."

We walked through the large double doors and I smiled at the coziness of the normal looking living room.

He motioned for me to sit down on the old worn couch. "I'll be right back."

I slid into the comfy couch and looked around the room. It was exactly as I remembered it. My lips formed into a smile. The lemonade, the photo album, Nicolai proposing… Wait. I sat straight up. Where were Nicolai and Snow? I had been so preoccupied by the devastation that surrounded me that I had completely pushed them to the back of my mind. My chest tightened as the panic began to set in.

Mathias returned holding an old tattered scroll. "Angelina, it's been quite a while, old friend."

"Tell me, Mathias, what's happened? Why is the world in such chaos, and where is Nicolai?"

Sadness filled his dull eyes as he sat down next to me. "There is something I must tell you."

"What?" I croaked.

"You did this," he uttered quietly.

My eyes widened in disbelief. "You must be mistaken. I don't remember doing any of this."

He nodded. "Yes, you did this. What you're seeing is a premonition."

My heart ached. "But why? I could never...I would never..."

He put his hand on top of mine and squeezed it reassuringly. "Angelina, he's returned."

"Who?"

There was a long pause before he finally uttered a name. "Tristan."

My mind searched for some sort of recognition. "Tristan?"

"Yes. You've met him before."

I was paralyzed by his words. "I have?"

He nodded and touched my forehead slightly with his index finger. "Remember?"

The memory of a cool breeze kissing my warm skin softly filled my mind. The old screen door opening, a devilishly handsome man with dark, shaggy hair and the most exquisite emerald green eyes walking in...

A gasp escaped my lips. "The man from the grocery store?"

"Yes."

"Why didn't he take me when he had the chance?"

"He knew Nicolai was watching."

"But why me?"

"Age-old rivalries and power, of course. Plus, I believe he's in love with you."

"In love with me?"

"Yes, but, Angelina, listen. Time is of the essence. He will try to trick you."

"What do I need to do?"

"He's already taken Laurana. Jeremiah will seek your aid. You must go with him despite what Nicolai says. Do you understand?"

My mind struggled to comprehend everything he was saying. "What could he possibly want with Laurana? Heck, what would anyone want with her?"

"She knows your weakness."

Then it hit me. "Nicolai," I said slowly.

He nodded. "Yes. Tristan knows if he can separate the two of you, he has a better chance of claiming your soul."

My hand instinctively covered my heart. "No. I won't allow it."

Mathias smiled. "There's the Angelina I know."

I studied my old friend. "Your eyes are so dull now, Mathias. What happened to you?"

He looked down shamefully. "I've done something terrible."

"What, Mathias? What have you done?"

"None of that matters right now." He looked back up. "If we don't stop Tristan, none of us will have a future." He placed his hand on mine and his eyes ran through a plethora of colors.

"Mathias, your eyes…they're changing!"

"Angelina, you're the key! You can change the future," he answered excitedly.

"The key to what?"

He smiled. "To our future, of course."

"I'm so confused. This might actually be worse than when I was trying to remember my past."

"I highly doubt that," he said.

"So, what do I have to do?"

"Once again, you'll be tasked with making a choice."

"What kind of choice?" I asked.

"You will face the hardest decision of your life. You must choose between those bound to you and the entire world."

My life consisted of always making some sort of choice. "But why, Mathias?"

"You were put on this earth to do some amazing things, Angelina, but sometimes life can be cruel. However, its cruelty shall be our salvation. You must decide, and though you may not want to…you must do it."

Images of Nicolai, Jeremiah, and my father filtered through my mind. Losing any one of them would devastate me. How could I possibly choose between them?

"If you do not make a choice, the death and destruction you've witnessed will come to pass. Angelina, you're the key to the future of the world. When the Crimson Moon rises, you must choose, and choose wisely. The fate of the world lies on your shoulders."

A thick mist began to roll inside the room, making it almost impossible to see. "Mathias, where are you?!" I called out frantically.

I heard a faint whisper. "Choose wisely, Angelina. Listen to your head and not to your heart."

Warm hands grabbed me by the shoulders, shaking me gently. I grew dizzy and struggled to breathe. The panic had finally taken full control of my body. The taste of death and darkness was bittersweet. I closed my eyes and let the darkness carry me away.

Chapter 3
Kidnapped

The strange hands held onto my wrists firmly as a faint, familiar voice yelled my name through the thick fog. "Angelina, wake up!"

"Nicolai!" I called out helplessly. "Where are you?"

His voice drew closer. "Angelina, you're dreaming. Wake up."

I opened my eyes and drew in a long breath of fresh air. Nicolai's orange-ember-colored eyes stared back at me in bewilderment. Snow whimpered and pawed at the side of the bed, her pure white fur standing on end.

"Nicolai? Where am I?" I stuttered. "Where's Mathias?"

He released his strong hold on my wrists. "Angelina, what are you talking about?"

There was a loud knock at the front door. My heart fluttered and my knees grew weak. I glanced at Nicolai before jumping up out of bed and throwing on my silk bathrobe.

"What are you doing?"

"I'm going downstairs to answer the door."

He gave me a stern look, but it was too late. I was already rounding the corner and skipping down the steps.

"Angelina, it's three in the morning, let me answer the door." He called out from the bedroom, heavy footsteps soon following behind me.

"Did you forget we live in the quiet town of Buffalo?" I asked, ignoring his plea. "I'm probably the scariest thing here."

Heavy fists pounded on the outside of the door again. I turned the lock and braced myself for the unexpected. Nicolai grabbed my shoulder softly and pulled me close. "Please, let me answer it."

Nodding, I took a step behind him. A gasp escaped my lips when I saw my childhood friend standing in our doorway. "Jeremiah?" I whispered. "You're here."

Jeremiah had carried the weight of Cole's, the wolf that had protected me since birth, death hard. We hadn't spoken since the terrible battle in the forest.

He fell to his knees. "Angelina, you have to help me…they've taken her."

I freed myself from Nicolai's grasp and rushed to Jeremiah's side. Mathias' predictions were coming true.

Nicolai gestured for me to come to him. "Angelina…"

There was a hint of jealousy in Nicolai's eyes, but watching my childhood friend suffer was far worse. We had grown up together. My mother had practically raised him as her own. "No, Nicolai, Jeremiah needs me."

His face embodied disappointment. "I see."

Frowning, I ignored his sarcastic remark and went to my friend. "Jeremiah, what happened?" I asked, inviting him inside.

He rose and stepped inside, and for a moment I saw the damaged kid I had grown up with. Worry and lack of sleep could be seen in the creases and dark circles under his eyes. His dirty blond hair was a mess, and his strong stature had been replaced by fear.

He grabbed my hands and held them to his. Tears filled his bright blue eyes.

"I don't know, Angelina. I had just come out of the tree line and was headed back to my house when I heard a bloodcurdling scream."

"Laurana?"

He nodded. "Yes. It was Laurana, my fiancée."

Those two ending up together still surprised both Nicolai and myself. The rumor was that Jeremiah was the first man she had ever fallen in love with. Hopefully love had changed her.

"I wasn't fast enough, Angelina. I just wasn't fast enough."

"Jeremiah…" I looked up at Nicolai. He stared back at me with concern in his eyes.

"He left a note," Jeremiah said, choking back the emotion in his strained voice. He fumbled inside his jeans pocket and pulled out a wadded piece of paper. He thrust it towards me. "It's for you."

My hand shook slightly as I took it from him. It amazed me how scared one person could be of one simple, wad of paper.

"Go on, read it," Jeremiah said.

Smoothing the wrinkled paper, I began to read it quietly out loud.

My dearest Angelina,

Crimson Moon

The time has come for our worlds to become one. The darkness below craves the life of your world, while I crave you and your soul. Come to the home of my enemies hidden within the Crimson Forest. Your Nicolai knows the way.

Tristan

Crumpling up the note, I tossed it into the fireplace and watched the flames lick at it hungrily. "What does he mean by 'Nicolai knows the way?' Do you happen to know this Tristan?" I asked.

Silence followed my question, so I asked again, "Do you know Tristan?"

The guilty look on his face gave him away. He shoved his hands into his pockets and quietly replied. "Yes, I know him."

"How?"

He shrugged. "Unfortunately, our paths crossed once when we were younger. You seem to know him also."

Averting my eyes, I focused my attention back on Jeremiah. "We'll get her back, I promise."

"What if it's too late?" he asked.

"Well, then we must hurry," I replied. "However, I need to know what we're dealing with first. Nicolai, tell me everything you know."

He pulled his hands out of his pockets and ran them through his dark, unruly hair. His lips formed into a tight, thin line. "Well," he began. "Tristan is an ancient evil that comes from the darkness below."

A chill ran down my spine. The darkness and I were well acquainted.

"He used a very powerful pendant to escape the darkness and find the beacon of light," he continued.

"The beacon of light?"

He nodded. "Yes, a beacon of light, Angelina. That beacon of light is you."

Silence filled the room.

"A beacon of light, Nicolai? What does that even mean?"

"Angelina, the energy in your soul is the brightest in the entire world. It's a beacon of light that Tristan would kill for."

"Then why doesn't he come here and try to take it from me?" I said.

"He can't. You're still alive. You would have to give it to him of your own free will."

The puzzle pieces finally started to come together. "So, that's why he wants me to come to him."

Nicolai looked at Jeremiah. The desperation in his voice was heavy. "You understand that Angelina can't go back into the forest, Jeremiah. He'll kill her."

I put my hands on my hips in defiance. "No, I'm going, and you can't stop me."

He shook his head. "Angelina, you can't risk your soul for Laurana."

Jeremiah balled up his fist and hit Nicolai square in the jaw. Nicolai stumbled backwards and smacked into the corner of the fireplace.

"Stop it!" I ordered. "Both of you stop it right now!"

Nicolai stood up and rubbed the side of his jawline. "You still hit like a girl."

"I would be careful saying that." Bethani's sweet voice chimed in as she skipped down the last few steps and plopped down on the couch. "You won't stop her from going. You both know that just as much as I do."

I was still glad she had moved in with us. She had not only kept her promise to watch over me, but had become my best friend, also.

The distinct look of disapproval graced Nicolai's handsome face. "Angelina, you can't do this," he persisted, "you just can't."

My words escaped me. I knew what I had to do to save Laurana and the world. The hard part was working up the nerve to do it.

Chapter 4
Friendship

"We need to come up with a plan," Jeremiah suggested.

Nodding, I picked up the phone to call my father.

Nicolai rushed to stop me. "Angelina, it's late. We can handle this in the morning."

"We don't have time for a debate." I pushed the familiar phone number into the keypad. "I need to call my father. He'll know what to do."

"Please." Nicolai begged, "Don't do this."

The phone rang on the other end of the line and I held my fingers to my lips to hush him. On the second ring, a groggy voice answered.

"Hello?"

"Father? I need to come over right away."

"Is everything alright, Angelina?" he asked.

"Something terrible is happening in the forest," I said in response to his question. I looked at the wooden clock above the mantle. 4:00 a.m. The sun would be coming up soon. "We don't have much time. I'll explain when we get there."

"Okay, I'll see you soon," he replied before hanging up the phone.

Looks of curiosity surrounded me.

Nicolai stepped in front of me in one last attempt to stop me from going into the forest. "Angelina, please?"

Pushing past him I headed up the stairs to put something a little more practical on. Though spring was fast approaching, the air still had a hint of winter chill which we needed to be prepared for. This wasn't going to be a normal trip into the forest. With the frigid air and the frozen ground, warmth was not going to come easy to us.

I skipped up the steps to my bedroom to change. A few moments later I was dressed in old comfy jeans, a long sleeved thermal shirt, and a gray, oversized hoodie. My mother had bought me the hoodie one Christmas after she saw me admiring it online. Though it was stunning, it also came with a stunning price tag of $59.99—something I could never afford on my own.

Admiring the softness of the vintage hoodie, I breathed in the faint aroma of my mother—lavender and vanilla. A lump formed in my throat at the thought of her. She had always been there for me through everything, and now she was gone when I needed her the most.

Sadness tugged at my heart. To quash it, I grabbed a hair tie and pulled my hair into a loose braid.

"Everything okay up here?"

Startled, I jumped at the sound of Nicolai's voice. "Everything's fine," I replied. "Pack warm, it's still going to be chilly out there."

There was an irritated look on his face. "I don't get chilled, Angelina."

"How could I forget?" I said.

He grabbed both of my arms. "You really need to reconsider doing this. The forest is not safe."

Pulling away from him, I yanked a black knitted hat from the top of the closet and put it on. "Nicolai, Jeremiah's our friend and he needs our help."

"No, he's *your* friend and he can help himself." I could tell by the disapproval on his face that this conversation wasn't going anywhere.

"Angelina…" he begged.

My hand rose to stop him, "No, Nicolai, perhaps you forgot who helped rescue me. How could you possibly forget that he was right by your side?" I slid a pair of black knitted gloves and slid them over my slim fingers. "It's our turn to help him now."

His stare was powerful, but I didn't let it sway my decision. Sighing, I smoothed my braided hair and faced him. "We have to do this. Nicolai, *I* have to do this."

Without another word, he sat down on the bed next to Snow, who was snoring loudly. His steady eyes studied me momentarily before looking down at the floor. "Everything in me tells me we shouldn't go into the forest."

"Nicolai, you know how important Laurana is to Jeremiah. He would do the same for you."

"But you're risking so much!"

"Look, I'm not going to argue with you over this. It's already settled. I'm going, with or without you."

He ran his hands through his dark hair in frustration. "You don't know Tristan. He's clever and calculating. He's aware of the power you possess to control life and death, and most importantly, he knows how to hurt you."

"Then maybe you should just stay here so he can't hurt me."

My words stung. The muscles in Nicolai's jaw twitched in silent retaliation to my comment. "What the hell is that supposed to mean, Angelina?"

My mouth opened, but no sound came out. Instead, I reached for the locket that hung loosely around my neck.

Nicolai stood up and pulled me into his warm embrace. "I just don't want to lose you," he said, "we've fought so hard for this."

He was right, we had fought hard for our love, but the world needed us. Hell, Laurana needed us. The possibility of losing those you love is the worst thing imaginable. I had to do everything in my power to save them, even if it meant losing my own soul in the process.

Chapter 5
Apologetic Love

Snow yawned lazily and hopped down off the bed. Her nails clicked across the hardwood floor as she trotted over to the doorway and sat down. She always kept a steady eye on me while I was with Nicolai. She had claimed me as part of her wolf pack from the moment she arrived on our doorstep as a little bundle of white fluff. Her instincts were beginning to kick in, and she had grown quite protective over me.

Turning my attention back to Nicolai, I gave him apologetic look. "I don't want to fight anymore."

Snow let out a warning growl to let Nicolai know she now had her sights set on him.

His brows shot up in amusement. "I think your wolf-dog is jealous of me."

"Ha!" I laughed. "She's not the only one with jealous tendencies in this household."

Nicolai caught my drift. "Yeah…about that…"

"It's okay," I said.

"It's just…" he flashed his charming smile, "You know what? I'm sorry. Please forgive my behavior tonight."

How could anyone reject someone with a smile like that? "Of course, I forgive you," I replied with a kiss. Snow growled in disapproval and I shooed her out the door and told her to go downstairs.

Nicolai released his hold on me and poked his head out the door to confirm she had indeed done as I'd asked. Two seconds later he gave me a thumbs-up. "She's gone. Now come here so I can apologize to you the right way."

He grabbed me by the waist and pulled me close. His warm skin felt good against mine.

"What if she comes back?" I joked.

"Well, if she does happen to come back, I guess I'll just have to show her who's boss, now won't I?"

"You? Show her who's boss?" I laughed. "I think it may be the other way around."

He smirked. "Yeah, she really doesn't like me too much, does she?"

"Nah, not really, so you had better be good to me, unless you want be eaten." I poked his chest and he grabbed my index finger, biting it gently.

"If you're not careful, I'm going to eat you."

A flirtatious grin spread across my face. "I'd like to see you try."

"I love you, Angelina."

The butterflies fluttered around in my stomach. "I love you, too."

"Well, I guess if we're going to do this, we should come up with a solid plan."

"You're right," I said. "We should get everyone together and head over to my father's house."

"Okay." He kissed me once more on the forehead. "I'll meet you downstairs."

He left the room and I caught a glimpse of myself in the mirror that hung on the back of the closet door. Tired chestnut-colored eyes stared back at me. The last adventure had nearly taken my life…a few times in fact, and now we were going back at it again. Another journey into the famous but deadly Crimson Forest. How deceiving it was with its mask of beauty and serenity.

Skipping down the steps, I tried to hide the fear that had begun to creep up on me from my companions. By the look of dismay on Bethani's pretty face, she already knew what was going on. She gave me a small nod as if to say everything was all going to be okay. Smiling, I nodded back. All eyes were now on me.

Jeremiah gave me a weak smile. "There she is."

"Yup, here I am," I said.

He pulled me in for a hug. "Thank you for doing this for me. You have no idea what it means."

His blue eyes were bloodshot and weary. I hugged him back and buried my head into his chest. He smelled like the forest—earthy and sweet. "Yes, Jeremiah, I do."

Nicolai let out a heavy sigh and disappeared into the kitchen.

"What's his problem?" Jeremiah asked.

Bethani grinned. "Oh, don't worry about him, he's just mad that you're cooler than he is."

My hand covered my mouth so Nicolai didn't hear the laugh that had escaped. A few moments later he returned, a smug look on his handsome face. "Are you guys ready to head out?" he asked.

Bethani bounded over to the front door. "Yes, I think we are."

Jeremiah's weary blue eyes were suddenly full of life. Vengeance fueled him. "Well then, let's go kick the shit out of that son of a bitch, Tristan."

"Yes, let's." I locked the door behind me. Snow let out a gruff woof and trotted next to me, wagging her tail happily. She was excited to go on her first big adventure.

"You're good, Snow," I said. She licked my hand and ran a short distance ahead to scout out the area. Our first stop was my father's house, which sat at the edge of town. After that, it was back into the Crimson Forest. My heart fluttered at the thought.

Bethani slowed down and nudged my shoulder. "The one who sacrifices the most is the one that will save the world."

"But haven't I already sacrificed enough?" I asked.

"You're still breathing, aren't ya?" she replied.

Though she had a point, it wasn't the thought of me dying that worried me. It was losing any one of them. I had already lost so much to the dangers that lurked within the forest. I simply refused to lose anyone or anything else, including my soul.

Chapter 6
Torture

Laurana's light eyes were bright with fury. "He'll come for me!"

"Oh, my dear Laurana, I'm counting on it." Tristan smiled viciously. "You know, some say that time is endless." Tristan paced back and forth in front of her. "However, your time is running out. What's Angelina's weakness?"

Laurana glared at him in hatred. "I don't know."

He nodded to something in the forest. "Mathias, come out."

Confusion washed over Laurana's face. "Mathias?"

A dark, shadowy figure emerged from the thick moss-covered brush. He lowered the hood on his jacket, revealing a head full of black hair and ice white skin. His red eyes stared straight ahead. "Yes?"

Laurana struggled to free herself from the tight binds that held her against the old ash tree. "Mathias, you traitor!"

Mathias looked down. "I'm not here by choice."

"I don't care why you're here," she said. "The point is, you're here."

Tristan clapped his hands together in amusement. "Oh, how cute!" He walked over and ran his finger down Laurana's smooth cheek. She turned her head in disgust.

"Don't touch me," she warned.

He looked at Mathias and back to Laurana. "I'm assuming you two know each other?"

"You traitor," she repeated, hatred in her bright eyes.

Mathias continued to stare at the ground. "What is it you want, Tristan?"

He nodded towards the pretty blonde. "Why don't we show this pretty little girl what happens when we don't cooperate."

"I refuse."

Tristan's brows shot up in surprise and he put his hand to his ear. "I'm sorry, what did you just say?"

Mathias stood his ground. "No, Tristan, not her."

Tristan let out a hearty laugh. "Aww, you really thought you were going to have a choice in the matter!"

Mathias looked up, his once-red eyes now a calm sea green. "I won't," he said.

Tristan cocked his head to the side and drew closer to Mathias. "Did you say…you won't?"

Mathias remained silent.

"I see," Tristan said. He began pacing back and forth in between them, his hands folded behind his back.

Laurana watched silently, trying her best to escape from her binds.

"Perhaps, you've forgotten why I've brought you here, Mathias. Maybe I should remind you."

Suddenly the apparition of a small boy appeared. He looked to be no older than maybe five years old. He opened his mouth to speak, but no sound came out.

Mathias ran to the apparition. The ghostly boy disappeared into thin air and Mathias fell to his knees. "My son!"

Tristan bent down and put his arm around the desperate man. "There, there Mathias. You'll get your son's soul back as soon as you've paid your debt."

Mathias shrugged Tristan's arm off him and stood back up. He slowly made his way over to Laurana and looked at her with apologetic eyes. "I'm sorry. This is something I must do." With that, he backhanded her across her face. She grinned at him, blood beginning to seep through the crevices of her perfect white teeth, "Angelina is going to hate you for this."

"She'll understand," he said as he hit her again.

"Will she, though?" Laurana flinched in anticipation of another backhand to the face, but it never came.

Mathias leaned close to her and whispered. "Just tell him what he wants to know, and this will all stop."

She flung her head forward and tried to bite him. "I'll never tell that asshole anything!"

Tristan covered his mouth in amusement and laughed. "By golly, I think she just called me an asshole!" He twirled his fingers and another apparition appeared. This time a tall, well-built man with blond hair appeared.

She stared at the illusion in horror. Her heart ached as she studied the tall, handsome man with the innocent smile. His blue eyes twinkled as he walked carelessly through the forest. She knew that face well. It was the only man she had ever fallen for and the father of her unborn child—Jeremiah.

A burst of raw emotion coursed through her. She felt helpless as she fought to hide her emotion from her enemy. She cursed silently to herself as a warm tear slid down her cool cheek. Tears were a sign of weakness, and damnit, she wasn't weak. "What are you doing?" she asked through clenched teeth.

Tristan mocked her sad face. "Aww, you poor, poor girl. Don't cry," he said, wiping away the rogue tear that had escaped down her cheek.

"Shut up!" she yelled.

Tristan nodded to Mathias and he hit her again.

She lifted her head wearily. "Leave Jeremiah alone," she warned.

"Or what?" he joked, running his finger through the specter. It rippled and a new image appeared. It was of Jeremiah and Angelina walking side by side down a crimson-covered path through the forest. A wicked smile spread across Tristan's face. Laurana's jealous reaction was exactly what he was looking for.

"I'm going to rip that smile right off your face," she promised. She felt a mind-numbing pain across her face again. "Is that all you got, Quasimodo?"

Tristan nodded and Mathias smacked her again, this time with such force, that she saw stars. She opened her swollen eyes and saw a lock of her long blonde hair was now highlighted with bloody streaks. "I've always wanted to be a redhead," she said, spitting out a mouthful of blood.

"This doesn't have to go on you know—all you have to do is tell me what I want to know," Tristan replied.

"Who are you anyways?" she asked. "Oh wait, let me guess, you're some jilted ex from her past life that had his heart broken because you weren't man enough."

Tristan's face went blank. Sadness filtered into his eyes, and awkward silence hung heavy in the air. In one swift moment, Tristan was suddenly standing nose to nose with her, his hand squeezing the sides of her face firmly.

Fear was a rare emotion for Laurana, but she felt it now. "I see I've struck a nerve," she said.

"You don't know anything!" he scoffed. "You're merely a small piece of a much bigger picture."

Laurana laughed loudly. "If you say so."

He squeezed her face tighter and she struggled to ignore the pain. "You're pathetic," he spewed, angrily, in her face. "Your species is no match for me."

Tristan released the grip on her face. Tears filled her eyes and she drew in a long sigh of relief. He turned around and dismissed the illusion angrily. "What, oh what, shall we do with your dear Jeremiah?"

She felt her stomach tie into knots. "Why are you doing this?"

"You see, Laurana, I've spent numerous years looking for Angelina. Any trace that she might be alive. Any signs that she still…" He put a finger to his chin as if he were deep in thought. "Existed," he finished.

"So, you are a jilted ex!" she said.

"Watch your tongue!" he warned.

"But you knew her before she was human," she replied matter-of-factly.

"I did," he said. "In fact, let me tell you a little story about the beginning of time."

Chapter 7
Time

The time of the Gods had come to an end. Christianity had taken over, and soon the mighty Gods became nothing more than a myth. Most of the Gods had taken refuge to a dimension beyond the stars to live in peace and watch humanity from afar. A select few stayed behind to continue their work maintaining the many souls death presided over in the darkness below.

Tristan's father, Hades, had been a God; a very powerful one, in fact. However, his mother had been a human. The Goddess Hecate had punished him cruelly for that. Relations with humans had been forbidden since the dawn of man. It was their most sacred law and violating it meant a fate worse than death. Though Hades was powerful, he was no match for the wrath and power of Hecate. She tortured his beloved wife in front of him before banishing her soul to a place some might consider to be Hell. She then banished Hades and his son to the darkness below for an eternity of soul reaping, a job not even the darkest of Gods wanted to do.

Tristan frowned at the lonely memories from his childhood. He had spent years trying to find a way to come back and make Hecate pay for destroying his family. Then one day, he was given a gift. The soul from a humanoid creature filtered into the darkness, lighting the entire area around them. This soul was the purest, yet most evil, soul he had ever come across. Even his father was taken aback by its bright light. He could still remember the look of terror on his father's face when he reached out to touch it.

"It can't be," Hades whispered.

"What is it father?"

He remembered the silence and the fearful look in his father's eyes.

"Son, don't touch it."

Ignoring his father, he reached up to touch the bright orb. "Why?" Tristan had scoffed, "What's it going to do, bite me?" And bite him, it did. A bolt of electricity shot straight through his body like a gunshot, instantly paralyzing him. The bright soul filtered in through his screaming mouth, sending small electric shocks to his heart. Then as the soul touched his, he felt peace and something more. Something simply amazing. It was genuine love. It swirled through him and he smiled faintly. He had never felt such a raw, beautiful form of emotion.

"Father, what was that?" he asked in awe.

Just as quick as it had come, the soul emerged from Tristan's body and disappeared into the darkness. His knees buckled and he hit the ground. His father rushed to his side.

"Tristan!"

Tristan opened his eyes warily. "Wow!" he said, breathlessly. "What just happened?"

His father let out a sigh of relief and shook his head. "That is the soul of something very powerful."

"But what could possess that much power?" Tristan asked.

"Only the soul of a God could possess such power."

"How does one even kill a God? I thought we were immortal."

"Good point son, unless"—his eyes widened in surprise—"a law was broken."

Tristan nodded. "Like you and Mother."

"Exactly."

"But who would violate the law? Especially after witnessing what happened to *us*." A bitter look fell upon Tristan's face.

"Someone who didn't think they would get caught," his father replied.

"We need to find out who it is. We can't continue to sit here and suffer in the darkness while someone else goes free."

His father put his hand on his shoulder and smiled. "Don't worry, son, we'll find out who did it, and we'll make it right."

Tristan stared into the darkness. The soul had been like a potent drug and one touch had him addicted. He wanted more and he would do whatever was in his power to get it. His wish came true when one of Laurana's ancestors journeyed into the darkness to find him. They knew of his desperation to return to the ground above to enact his revenge, and they knew he had the gift of being able to see a soul within a body. It was his gift they needed, and all he had to do in return to gain his freedom was bring them a child. Not just any child, but one whose soul was both dark and light. He was determined to find the child—and find the child he did.

Chapter 8
Deadly Innocence

Laurana looked at him warily. "So, you found the child, and...?"

"And the child just so happened to be the daughter of Hecate."

"Angelina?"

"Hers had been the soul that had filtered into the darkness. She is both dark and light. She's the most powerful being to ever exist." Tristan looked off into the distance, suddenly rattled by the thought.

Laurana, noticing his sudden fear, took full advantage. "You're afraid of her," she said knowingly.

He was quiet and continued to stare off into the distance.

"She's going to kill you, Tristan, and deep down, you know it to be the truth."

He swung around and hit her himself, pure evil on his handsome face. "Shut up! You have no idea how long I've waited for this moment!"

She struggled to lift her head. "Why didn't you destroy her when you had the chance? As a child?"

His features grew softer and he looked at her thoughtfully. "You see, when I came across the child, I immediately noticed her odd-colored eyes. They were the color of an early morning sunrise—burnt orange with beautiful bright speckles of red scattered throughout them. At that moment, I was certain she was not only human, but one of you—the Ad'Noki."

The Ad'Noki was what Tristan had called them since the beginning of time. They were an ancient species whose only goal was to live in peace below the earth and simply be unknown to the world around them. They were very deadly if disturbed. His father had warned him to stay far away from their kind, and that, coming from a God, was enough to make his skin crawl.

Laurana gasped. She hadn't heard that term in a very long time. Very few knew their name, and those who did, stayed clear of their kind.

"Surprised?" He laughed. "You see, my pretty friend, my father warned me of your race. When I came upon the little girl playing in the forest with her black wolf pup, looked upon her beautiful eyes, and saw the colors of her soul, I knew I couldn't follow through with my part of the deal."

She suddenly understood. "Because you wanted her for yourself."

He smiled wickedly. "Smart girl, but you see, I couldn't take her at that very moment because someone else was with her."

"Who?" she asked.

"None other than my longtime nemesis, Hecate."

Mustering up her strength, she lifted her head to look at him, defiant. "Hecate is our sacred goddess."

He let out a bone chilling laugh. "Your most sacred goddess." He ran his finger down the side of her bloody face. "You see, Laurana, this is the perfect time, not only can I claim Angelina's soul, but I can finally get my revenge on your goddess for destroying my family."

Hatred filled Laurana's bright eyes. "She will destroy you and what's left of your family."

"That's where you're wrong, my dear. You see, Hecate is forbidden from seeing her daughter. That was her punishment for cross breeding with your species. Quite unfair, don't you think?"

"But she didn't breed with a human."

He balled up his fist and acted as if he was going to hit her. She flinched in anticipation of pain, but he lowered his arm and sighed. "No, but she still broke the rules. Her punishment should have been far worse."

"And so here you are. What perfect timing," she said sarcastically.

A smile returned to his rugged face. "Here I am, but there's still one little problem." Annoyed, he kicked at the ground.

"Nicolai," Laurana said.

"Yes, Nicolai." His eyes were full of envy. "If he hadn't followed her through to this life, she would've already been mine."

Mathias, who had been watching silently, finally chimed in. "Angelina doesn't know what she's capable of nor the power she possesses. He is simply protecting her."

"Protecting her?" He grinned. "He is letting her power go to waste!"

"She's weak," Mathias said quietly. "She may never fully recover her power."

"Her mind is weak because she was reborn a human," Tristan corrected. "Angelina herself is NOT weak."

Mathias looked at the ground and didn't utter another word.

"So, tell me, Laurana, what is her weakness?"

"Shouldn't you already know?" she said. Her voice was heavy with sarcasm. "I mean, you are the son of a God after all."

"That is the one thing I am unable to see, and thus why you are here." He pointed to her binds and chuckled. "Now be a good girl and answer my question."

At that moment, Laurana knew Tristan would do anything to claim Angelina. He had tasted both life and death within Angelina's soul, and there was nothing she was going to be able to do to stop him. There was only one way to protect Jeremiah and her baby, and that meant revealing a secret that could end the life of someone she considered a friend.

Chapter 9
Pain

The time had come for Laurana to confess. "Fine, if I tell you Angelina's weakness, will you spare Jeremiah's life?"

He nodded.

"Swear it," she hissed.

"I swear that I shall not lay a finger on your dear Jeremiah."

She lowered her head in defeat. "Fine, I'll tell you."

"Marvelous!" He clapped his hands again. "Do tell, I'm quite eager to know."

She sighed. "Nicolai."

"Wait, are you saying…"

"Nicolai is her weakness," she answered shamefully.

"I should've known," he whispered quietly to himself. "All this time, the answer was right in front of me."

"Now, let him go," she begged. Tears filled her swollen eyes. "Please, don't harm Jeremiah, he's all I have."

He ignored her and turned to Mathias. "Find them and bring them to me."

She pulled at her binds. "You promised you wouldn't hurt him!"

"I promised you *I* wouldn't hurt him." He laughed. "I never said *he* couldn't."

"No!" she screamed.

He glared at her. "Now, shall we finish this?" he asked, snapping his fingers.

"There's nothing worse you could do to me than take away the only man I've ever loved," she answered sharply.

"Is that so?" He laughed, motioning towards the forest.

She watched in horror as two long strands of crimson moss snaked towards her along the ground. "No," she whispered.

"I once heard a story that when your species dies, your blood is drained and returned to the earth. Is that true?" he asked in amusement.

She spat at him, blood mucus spraying across his face. "They'll come for you, and they'll make you pay."

"Let them come and we'll see who makes who pay." He pointed to the moss. "Now, my dear Laurana, why don't we return you to the earth as you came?" He made a swift motion directing the long strands of moss to rise into the air. She struggled to break free of her binds. "Tell your ancestors I said hello."

She let out a bloodcurdling scream as he motioned for the moss to attack her. The long red strands bore into her pale skin like hot needles. A burning sensation spread up her legs and around her muscles. She desperately tried to free herself from her binds, but she was weak and the moss had reached her lungs. The moss was hungry for her blood. Gasping for air, she felt the sharp tendrils tear into them.

"Please," she let out a strangled plea, "my child."

"A child?"

She nodded, blood filling the whites of her eyes.

Amused, he replied, "I'll make sure to tell your dear Jeremiah that his daughter looked just like you."

A bloody tear fell down her cheek and she looked up to the sky. Blood gurgled in her lungs.

"Aww," he walked over and smeared the bloody tear across her face. "Are you hoping your goddess will save you?"

She ignored him and continued staring into sky. She winced in pain as the crimson moss finished feeding off her blood.

He pushed her blood-streaked hair behind her ear and whispered, "Your goddess doesn't care about you."

Laurana's eyes met his and she smiled weakly. "You're wrong about that," she managed to croak.

He raised his brow. "Oh, am I?"

"Yes, in fact, she told me to give you a message."

He took a step back and glared at her in suspicion. "Oh really, and what would this message be?"

"She's coming for you, and this time she's taking your heart back with her." Laurana grinned evilly, baring blood-stained teeth before letting out a final breath. Her head fell limply to the side and everything grew quiet.

"Nothing can stop me now." Tristan smiled as the moss snaked out of Laurana's mouth and continued spiraling its way up the tree. "Not even you, Hecate," he muttered, glancing up at the misty morning sky above him.

Chapter 10
Beautiful Death

The gravel path that led from the forest to town was a welcome sight. We quickened our pace, and before we knew it, we were standing in front of Tom's Tavern.

Bethani looked at me, worry on her face. "Angelina, are you okay?"

The nausea hit with overwhelming speed. I draped my arm over my stomach and bent down in pain. Nicolai was by my side in an instant.

"What's wrong?" he asked.

"I…I don't know," I stammered.

"Maybe she's pregnant," Jeremiah mumbled under his breath just loud enough for everyone to hear.

Nicolai's eyes widened and I couldn't help but laugh out loud. "I'm not pregnant."

Jeremiah rolled his eyes. "That you know of."

"Whatever." I closed my eyes as the pain increased. An image of Laurana, bloody and covered in crimson moss, entered my mind. "No, that can't be real," I whispered. The moss snaked in and out of her mouth as her desperate eyes stared into mine.

Nicolai's voice faltered. "Angelina, what is it?"

Laurana's loud scream filled my ears. "Help me!" she mouthed.

"How?" I asked the horrific image.

Nicolai wrapped his strong arms around my hunched over body. "How what?" he asked. "Angelina, you're scaring us."

"Kill me," Laurana begged. "Please, don't let me suffer."

Warm tears escaped my eyes. "I can't."

"Angelina?" Nicolai called out helplessly.

Her voice engulfed my mind. "Kill me," she repeated.

My index finger began to subconsciously draw an invisible x into the air. "Death," I whispered, and Laurana's pleas grew silent. Her face disappeared from my mind and the so did the agonizing pain I shared with her. I sat up, dizzy by my escapade.

Bethani nodded at me in approval. "You did the right thing."

"You know?" I asked.

She put her hand on my shoulder and squeezed it lightly. "Yes, I know."

"How can it be the right thing if I ended her life?"

"Because you let her die in peace."

Overhearing our conversation, Jeremiah walked over and put his hands on his hips. "Who died in peace?"

I couldn't look at him. How was I supposed to tell him I had just killed the woman he loved? I looked to Bethani for help.

"Jeremiah," she turned to face him, "Laurana's dead."

His mouth dropped open. "What did you just say?" he asked in disbelief.

There was a blank expression on Bethani's innocent face. "You heard me right the first time," she said.

He looked at me helplessly. "Wait, Laurana's dead?"

"Angelina saved her from an agonizing death. You should thank her."

"Thank her?" he repeated.

Bethani nodded.

His voice grew louder. "You're saying I should thank her for killing my fiancée? The woman that was meant to be my wife? The woman who was carrying my child."

I stared at him in horror. "No."

Awkward silence filled the air. Nicolai stared at the faces around him. "Jeremiah, you can't blame her, she didn't know."

"She did the right thing," Bethani reiterated.

Jeremiah made a fist and punched the wooden telephone pole that stood beside him. "Why does everything I love get taken away from me?!" He hit the pole again, sending shards of wood splintering onto the ground.

I stood up and my legs quivered beneath me. Somehow, I managed to stumble to my friend's side. "Jeremiah, life can be cruel. There are things that will happen to us that we will never understand, but blaming me or yourself will get us nowhere."

An angry cry escaped his lips. "But I loved her, Angelina, I loved her."

"She knows that," Bethani chimed in.

He looked up at her with a puzzled look on his face. "How do you know?"

She pointed to a faint shadow in the distance.

Knowing of Nicolai's keen eyesight, Jeremiah looked to him for help. "Is it her?" he asked.

Nicolai studied the image and nodded. "What Bethani claims is true."

Without hesitation, Jeremiah took off running towards her. "Laurana!"

Laurana held up her hand and he stopped a few inches from her. "Jeremiah, can you hear me?" Her mouth was unmoving, yet he could hear her voice.

Tears filled his eyes. "Yes, my love, I can hear you." He looked at the small bundle in her arms. "Is that…?"

She nodded. "Don't be sad." She reached out and caressed his cheek. "We are at peace."

"Did Tristan do this to you?" he asked angrily.

She nodded once again. "And there's a traitor hiding in your midst."

"Who is it?" he demanded.

"I cannot tell you, as his fate is his own, and he must answer for the choices he has made."

"He?"

Laurana smiled. "My love, death calls to each of us at our own time. When it does, we have no choice but to answer."

"But our child," he said.

"I know." She pulled the blanket back slightly. "She's beautiful."

The color left his face and his electric-blue eyes widened in surprise. "She?"

"Yes, come." She motioned for him to come closer.

The color filtered back into his face and a warm smile appeared as two sleepy, little electric-blue eyes peered up at him.

"She has your eyes," she pointed out.

He reached out to touch the little bundle in her arms but stopped the moment he heard a faint cry. "Was that…?"

She smiled warmly. "Yes, that came from her."

"Is she okay?"

"She knows you're near and is upset that you cannot hold her."

"I want to hold her so badly," he cried out. "I want to let her know that her daddy is here to protect her and keep her away from all the evils of the world."

Laurana's spectral image began to grow lighter and her voice grew faint. "She already knows."

Desperation filled Jeremiah's eyes. "Wait!" he called out, motioning for her to stop.

She looked up at the sky and back at him. "We must go, we are being called home."

"Please, don't go," he begged.

"We will see each other again, my love. This I promise to you, but for now, we must return home with our ancestors."

He grabbed the knife from his boot holster and held it firmly against his throat. "Then I will return with you."

"No," she held up her hand, "you will not do any such thing."

"My life without the two of you will be nothing but a life of emptiness."

Her eyes narrowed. "Jeremiah listen to me; your job on this earth is not over yet. Even if you were to slice your own throat, you would not die, as death is not yet ready to call you home.

Blood trickled down his neck from the pressure of the blade. "But it's the only way we can be together," he said.

"We will be together soon enough," she promised.

"Please don't ask me to travel this world without you, I can't do it alone." he begged.

"Jeremiah, yes, you can. You are the master of your destiny. You must seek out Tristan and kill him before the Crimson Moon rises."

"Why is he doing this?" I called out behind him.

Laurana looked past Jeremiah and her eyes met mine. "You know who he is, Angelina, all you have to do is remember."

I frowned. "So, we're back to this *remembering* crap."

She narrowed her eyes in annoyance. "Angelina, he's coming for you, and he will not stop until you are his.

Her image grew faint. "We must go."

He dropped the knife and reached out to her. "I will find him, Laurana," Jeremiah promised, "and I will kill him."

Her voice was barely a whisper. "I love you, Jeremiah. In fact, I've loved you from the first moment I met you."

He reached out to caress her face but was met by a cool breeze that rushed through his empty fingertips. Her spirit was returning to a place he could not follow her to, but in his heart, he knew they would once again be reunited when the time was right.

The realization of Laurana's death weighed on each of us heavily as we listened to the faint cry of a newborn drifting through the gentle breeze above us. I looked at Jeremiah, saddened by the events that had just taken place. That moment, I knew I had to make Tristan pay for the pain he had caused my friend.

Chapter 11
Daniel's Song

I knocked on my father's door feverishly until he answered it. There was a worried look on his youthful face. I pushed past him.

"What's wrong?" he asked.

"You must come with us now," I urged. "There's no time to waste."

"Aren't you going to tell me what's going on?"

I pushed him out the door. "We can tell you on the way," I said.

He raised his eyebrow in suspicion. "It's that urgent?"

"It's that urgent," I said.

He stumbled down the front steps. "Very well then."

Bethani, who happened to be standing at the bottom of the steps, embraced him with a friendly hug. "Well, hey there, Mr. Adams!" She flashed him her charming smile. "Long time, no see!"

He chuckled. "You're right, Bethani. It has been quite a while."

"You're looking as young as ever." She giggled. "Did you shave?"

He stroked his smooth chin and smiled. "Ah, you noticed!"

Her lavender eyes sparkled in amusement. "Of course I did." She nodded.

My father changed the subject. "So, why the big rush?"

I looked at him solemnly. "Laurana is dead."

The smile left his face. "Dead?"

Looking past him, I stared at the crimson-colored tree line. "Yes, and I believe her body is in there."

"Angelina, why would someone want to kill Laurana? Sure, she's not the nicest creature to walk the planet, but she had no enemies that I knew of."

Bethani coughed and motioned towards Jeremiah.

"Oh, I didn't mean to imply that she was unlikeable…" he muttered.

Jeremiah kicked a pebble down the stone driveway. "It doesn't matter, she's dead now, remember?"

Glancing over at my sullen friend, I grimaced. "Father, he did it to get to me."

"He?"

Just saying his name made me want to vomit. "Yes, Tristan," I replied.

He looked at me sharply. "What did you just say?"

By the look on his face, I knew he recognized the name. "I said Tristan. Do you know of him?"

He ignored my question and began walking briskly down the driveway. "We have to go."

Running to catch up with him, I noticed we were headed back to town. My companions could be heard not far behind me. "Wait, you know him?" I repeated.

He stopped and turned back towards me slowly. "I knew he would find you, Angelina. I just knew it."

"You do know him!"

"We don't have much time. If the Crimson Moon rises, all we know of this world will be lost."

My father turned to Nicolai, who had been standing quietly near a neatly stacked woodpile. "We may want to involve Daniel."

Nicolai gave him a cautious look. "It's too risky."

My interest was piqued. "Who's Daniel?" I asked.

They both ignored me. "He would be a powerful ally," my father said, trying to state his case.

Nicolai shook his head in disagreement. "No, Josiah, we can't bring Daniel into this."

"We'll be careful."

Nicolai shook his head again. "No."

"Hey! Both of you, stop it," I demanded. Crossing my arms angrily, I took a firm stance. "One of you had better tell me what's going on."

My father held his finger up. "One second, Angelina, this is important."

Hurt by his "hush," I zipped my lips.

"You know he can help us, Nicolai, and he'll keep her safe."

Nicolai grew quiet and by the look on his face, I knew he was deep in thought.

"Maybe you're right, Josiah." He finally nodded in agreement. "Let's go find Daniel."

Chapter 12
Crush

Something tugged at the back of my mind. I had heard the name Daniel before. Where had I heard it...then it hit me. "Are you talking about Daniel the mechanic?"

Surprised, they both looked at me in unison.

"Angelina, how do you know Daniel?" my father asked suspiciously.

I shrugged. "We live in Buffalo, a town with the population of 657 people. Not many people here go unnoticed."

His eyes narrowed and he gave me a stern look. "Can please you clarify?"

"Clarify what?"

"That you know him, or that you only know of him?" he said.

Sighing, I rolled my eyes. "Does it matter? We don't have time for this." I replied.

"Yes, in fact, it does matter."

Nicolai moved from the woodpile he had been leaning against. He took my hand in his and tilted my face up to look at him. "Angelina, please, this is important."

My stubbornness immediately melted away. "I only know of him. Marie, my high school best friend, used to have a crush on him, okay?"

"But you've never personally met him or talked to him?" Nicolai asked.

I tried to look away, but he held my chin firmly. "We walked past his shop one day while he was working on an old truck outside. Marie saw him with his shirt off and thought he was hot. We never actually talked to him."

Nicolai let go of my chin and gently kissed my forehead. His cool lips felt good against my warm skin. "Thank you, my love. That's all we needed to hear."

My father turned back towards town. "We should hurry."

I threw my hands in the air angrily. "Are you kidding me? You're not going to tell me anything?"

"We will tell you when you're ready, Angelina. Until then, there is nothing to tell you," my father said.

Bethani came up behind me and squeezed my shoulder softly. "Listen to them, they know what's best."

Sighing, I followed behind them. "All these stupid secrets are going to drive me mad."

She gave me a gentle push and laughed. "We're all mad here," she quoted.

Bethani always knew what to say to make me laugh. "*Alice in Wonderland*, really?"

"What?" She shrugged. "It fit the moment."

Laughing again, I motioned for Jeremiah to follow us.

"What's the plan?" he asked, jogging up to us.

"Apparently, we're headed into town to talk to Daniel."

"The mechanic?" he asked.

Nodding, I smiled sarcastically. "Maybe he's a magic mechanic."

A smile finally broke through his sullen face. "Maybe he has a magic wrench that could magically fix everything."

"I sure hope so," I replied, laughing again. It was good to see him smile.

We made our way back to town in silence. Daniel's shop sat just south of my father's house, only a short distance away. A few moments later, sweet music filled the air.

"Is that Elton John I'm hearing?" My father called out.

A man in a dirty blue grease monkey uniform emerged from under the front end of a beat-up old Ford pickup truck. "Is that Josiah's voice I hear questioning my taste in music?" he asked.

Laughing, my father walked over and shook the man's dirty hand. "Well, I would prefer Billy Joel's rendition of this song, but I suppose this is alright."

Daniel dropped the metal wrench he had been using and it hit the ground with a loud *clang*. He slammed the heavy truck hood. "What brings you to this side of town, old man?" he asked, wiping his greasy hands on his overalls.

My father's voice grew serious. "Tristan has returned."

Daniel stopped wiping his hands and stared at my father momentarily before picking up his tool box. "I see. What's our time frame?"

"I'm not quite sure yet, but I would guess we don't have much time," he replied.

Daniel's dark, serious eyes met mine. He was a handsome man, in a rough sort of way. His large, dirty hands matched his muscular frame and chiseled face. Narrowing my eyes, I tried to decide if that was stubble on his tan skin or just grease and grime.

"Why the odd expression?" he asked roughly.

"Nothing."

He smirked, shoving his hands into the pockets of his overalls. "Nothing, huh."

Nicolai, amused by their exchange of words interjected, "It's obvious she doesn't remember you, Daniel."

"I like how you talk about me like I'm not right here, Nicolai," I said.

"She hasn't regained all of her memories yet, and it's best we keep it that way," Nicolai warned.

"Maybe you're right, Nicolai. I bet she hasn't regained all her memories, including some of them that involved you," he replied, sarcasm heavy in his deep voice.

Nicolai didn't utter another word. My father stepped in between them and once again hushed me before I could ask another question. "Look, there's no time for bickering. We have to get to Tristan before time runs out."

Daniel picked up the wrench he had dropped earlier and threw it into his rusty toolbox. "Why did you come here anyways? It's not like I can help you."

Nicolai took a step forward. "You can help keep her safe—"

My father finished Nicolai's sentence for him. "—and we need you to find him."

He sighed and ran his hands through his dark, messy hair. "Tell me, Josiah, what's in this for me?"

Jeremiah spoke up suddenly. "Why does there have to be something in it for you? This guy killed my fiancée."

"And your point is?"

Jeremiah made a fist and lunged towards him. Nicolai stepped in between the two of them and held his hands up. "Woah, fellas." He pushed them apart and frowned. "Now, Daniel, we go way back. If I recall, you owe me a favor."

Daniel made a disgusted face and sighed again. "Well, damn."

"So, you'll help us?" I asked, hopeful for a new ally.

"I'll help him," he answered, glancing back up at Nicolai, "only because I owe him."

"Wow, aren't you charming," I commented under my breath. I felt his sharp gaze upon me and shrugged. "What?"

Without saying another word, he opened the door that had "Office" spray-painted across the top of it and went inside, slamming it shut behind him.

Jeremiah smirked. "Way to piss him off, Angelina."

"What?" I asked again with a shrug.

He shook his head, the smirk still gracing his handsome face. "Oh, Angelina…"

A few moments later, Daniel reemerged from the doorway. I felt my mouth drop open as he made his way towards us.

Bethani's sweet voice chimed up behind me. "I must admit, you clean up quite nicely."

He had cleaned the grit off his face, revealing his smooth, clean-shaven face. His dark hair was still a mess, but in a sexy sort of way. His ripped jeans hugged every muscle, while the buttons on his blue checkered flannel shirt struggled to stay in place.

"I believe you have a staring problem, miss." He walked past me, brushing against me as he went by. I blushed and caught a look of amusement on Nicolai's face, which confused me. If anything, I expected him to be jealous, not amused.

"Shall we be on our way?" he asked without turning around.

"Lead on," my father called out behind him.

"How can he possibly know where Tristan is?" I whispered to Nicolai.

"Let's just say he can see things others can't," he said.

"What does he see?"

Daniel's deep voice boomed out from up ahead. "I see everything."

"Alrighty then," I nodded, "let's go."

Nicolai motioned for me to go ahead of him. "After you, beautiful."

I had no idea where he was leading us, but I assumed it wasn't going to be somewhere pleasant. My father and Nicolai trusted him, so I supposed I should too; after all, we needed him to help us find Tristan before anyone else ended up dead. Our secret lives had been tucked away, out of the minds of the townsfolk, and I had to do everything in my power to keep it that way.

Chapter 13
Beautiful Magic

Ctephanyi smiled and set down her cup of tea. The butterflies fluttered past her and landed gracefully on the flowers that ran along the edges of her garden. She drew in a deep breath in and let it out slowly. She had gotten used to this life—this…human life. It had been difficult and awkward at first, but after time she had begun to like it.

Human life was simple, pleasant, and well…simple. Her day consisted of tending to her flower bed and watching other humans pretend to like each other as they passed one another on the street. Occasionally Nicolai and Angelina would surprise her with a visit. They would have a pleasant conversation that generally ended with her in tears thanking Angelina once again for giving her a second chance at life.

She frowned and ran her finger delicately across the top of her cup. She had been such a terrible person before, filled with spite and hatred. Her soul had been ugly and unforgiving. She didn't miss those feelings one bit and prayed every day that those feelings never returned. There was one thing she missed however. It was her husband, Elias. He had disappeared shortly after she had been turned human, and she hadn't seen him since. Occasionally, she thought she felt his presence nearby, but dismissed it as the simple human emotion—hope.

Today, she had awoken with a new feeling. Her entire body tingled, and she couldn't dismiss the overwhelming feeling that she was being watched. The cool breeze carried the familiar scent of lilac and lavender. It was the scent of her Goddess, Hecate. She turned around, and to her surprise, Hecate was standing behind her.

"Greetings, Ctephanyi."

The small glass trembled under her fingertips. "Hecate, to what do I owe this honor?" she asked, trying to hide the nervousness in her voice.

Hecate smiled and walked towards her. Her white dress shimmered in the sun while her long, dark hair swayed freely across her bare back. "I'm here to restore your power," she said.

Ctephanyi felt her face twist into a look of surprise. "You're giving me back my power?"

"That is correct," she answered. She nodded to the chair at the table. "May I?"

Ctephanyi nodded and cleared her throat. "I'm so sorry, where are my manners?" She pointed to the chair in front of her. "Please, have a seat."

Hecate smiled. "Thank you."

She pulled the chair out and sat down, revealing her bare feet as she crossed her long, slender legs. "It has come to my attention that one of my enemies has resurfaced and is going to attempt to take my daughter. This," she glared at Ctephanyi with hatred in her eyes, "cannot happen."

Ctephanyi stared at her in awe. "Why have you come to me? You're by far more powerful than I am."

Hecate raised a hand to silence her. "I am no longer allowed to help humans, but"—she smirked— "I *can* restore what was rightfully yours in the first place."

A silent understanding crossed between the two of them.

"I see," Ctephanyi said. She ran her finger around the brim of the cup again and frowned.

"You're afraid your new human emotions will get in the way."

She nodded and fought back the weakness that had begun to fill her eyes. "What if I fail you? What if I fail her?"

Hecate reached out and patted Ctephanyi's arm tenderly. "You won't allow yourself to fail me or her."

A warm tear escaped down her cheek and she nodded. "What do I need to do?"

Hecate smiled and gently wiped away the tear from Ctephanyi's face. "Find my daughter and keep her safe."

"Who is this enemy, Hecate? Why has he come for her?"

Her face grew dark and sullen. "His name is Tristan, and he seeks revenge for the punishment I bestowed upon his family for breaking our most sacred law."

Ctephanyi felt her eyes grow wide with fear. "Everyone knows of this story."

"So, you can imagine his hatred for me then."

She nodded. "That I can."

"Angelina must not give in to him. If the Crimson Moon rises, the world as you know it will cease to exist."

Ctephanyi knew if Tristan managed to get to Angelina, destruction would follow suit. She had been given a second chance at life, and if there was one way she could repay Angelina for that precious gift, then keeping her safe from Tristan was it.

Hecate lowered her voice and stared into Ctephanyi's eyes. "I will warn you," Hecate said, "he will try and tempt you with what you most desire."

She felt her heart flutter. "Elias?" she assumed.

Hecate nodded. "Yes, you must be prepared, for your heart is now human and there is no greater emotion than that of love."

She swallowed the knot that had begun to form in her throat. "I won't fail you," she promised.

"I know you won't." She smiled, smoothing the wrinkles from her dress as she stood up.

"My powers, will they…"

"Oh, yes!" Hecate chuckled, "I almost forgot." She pointed to the cup of tea in front of Ctephanyi, "Drink up, I hear tea is good for the soul." She walked away, her silky hair fluttering in the breeze behind her.

Ctephanyi stared at the cup in front of her. She knew what that tiny little teacup held inside. She picked it up and breathed in its leafy fragrance. "Well, here goes nothing." She took a long drink and set the cup back down on the table. Hoping to feel something, she frowned in disappointment. She felt absolutely nothing. In fact, the tingling sensation she'd felt earlier had ceased completely. Maybe it was too late, maybe she had been human for too long, and her body had simply rejected her magic.

A silky black and tan butterfly drifted lazily towards her before setting down on the edge of her cup. She admired its beauty. Its large, delicate wings flapped back and forth while its antennae flicked in silence. She held out her finger and without hesitation the creature floated from the cup to her finger. Its wings spread open and its antennae stood erect. She felt something brush against the side of her face and turned to see another large butterfly rest on her shoulder. Before she knew it, she became engulfed in a swarm of beauty. Soft wings fluttered against her cheeks, while antennae tickled her face. Her power had returned and nature trusted her once again. Now she could do exactly what she had promised to do—protect Angelina and save the world.

Chapter 14
Apologies

My father put his strong hand on Daniel's shoulder and laughed. "Those were the days, weren't they?"

Daniel smirked and nodded. "Yeah, they sure were."

"Aww, now don't you act like you didn't have fun back then, son."

I watched Daniel's smirk turn into a full-blown smile as he shrugged. "Yeah, I guess so."

Nicolai walked beside them and laughed. "Hey, do you remember that time we were all…"

I rolled my eyes and tuned them out. "Men," I grumbled.

"What's the matter? Jealous?" Jeremiah snickered behind me.

"Why in the world would I be jealous?" I asked, narrowing my eyes. "I don't care that they're taking time out to walk down memory lane."

He nudged me slightly and grinned. "Then why roll your eyes?"

I felt my cheeks flush in embarrassment. "I don't know." I shrugged. "Maybe because they seem to know him well, but I've never been introduced."

"Is that the real reason or is it because of the tension between you and Nicolai?"

I let out a heavy sigh. "I just don't know what his problem is lately."

"Why not ask him then?"

I looked down thoughtfully. "I've been so focused on the task at hand, I haven't…"

"I'm sorry," Jeremiah interrupted.

I looked up at him confused. "For what? You haven't done anything wrong."

He stopped in his tracks. "Yes, I have."

"Jeremiah…"

"Listen, Angelina. I killed Cole, and there's nothing I can do to bring him back."

"You didn't know…"

"It doesn't matter. His blood is on my hands and now karma has come full circle. A life for a life. Laurana for Cole."

"Is that what you think? Jeremiah, every soul on Earth is here for a certain amount of time. Once that time has expired, and they have done the task that was put before them, they get called to a greater place."

He stared at me thoughtfully, his beautiful blue eyes brimming with tears. "What was Laurana's task, Angelina? To die because she fell in love with me?"

"No." I gave him a sympathetic smile. "Her task was to simply love you when you needed love the most."

He wrapped his strong arms around me. "Angelina, I miss her so much."

I smiled and hugged him back. "I know."

"Please"—he squeezed me tighter—"talk to Nicolai. Don't let whatever is festering between the two of you get any worse." He released his grip and pulled away. "Don't take the time you have with him for granted. Before you know it, it will be gone."

I noticed Nicolai had stopped talking to my father and was staring at Jeremiah and me. He had a jealous, but also curious, look on his face.

Daniel stopped and frowned. "Are you slackers coming or what?"

I gave him a dirty look. "I really don't know why, but I don't like that guy. He's like an annoying brother that just won't go away."

Jeremiah chuckled. "Well he seems to like you."

"Pshh, yeah right." I punched him playfully in the arm.

His bright blue eyes twinkled while he acted as if the innocent hit was going to cause him to lose his balance. "Ouch!"

Bethani giggled as she walked past us. "She's been working out."

I laughed and tugged at his shirt. "Come on, *slacker*," I replied, trying to mimic Daniel's deep voice.

"Careful tugging on that shirt, you might just unleash some rippling muscles."

I made a gagging noise and he playfully punched me back. It felt good to joke around with him again. Looking forward, I caught Daniel staring at me with an odd expression on his face. He turned away and began walking ahead of our group the moment our eyes met.

"That guy is just weird," I muttered to myself.

"Before you judge him, maybe you should get to know him a little better," Bethani said, without turning around.

I nodded, embarrassed by my actions. I had forgotten about Bethani's keen sense of hearing. That girl could hear a mouse fart from three rooms away.

The Crimson Forest was only a short distance ahead of us. The summer breeze sifted through the trees, causing the leaves to flutter back and forth lazily. I looked down and admired the soft crimson moss as it snaked along the ground and up the tree trunks. How deceiving this place was, with its mask of beauty and serenity.

My attention to the forest was suddenly averted as a low rumble vibrated through the soles of my tennis shoes. Bending down on one knee, I placed my hand against the ground firmly. I held one finger up and motioned for my companions to be still.

"What are you doing?" Daniel asked, annoyed.

"Shh," I brought my finger to my lips and hushed him. "Do you feel that?"

Bethani bent down and placed her hand next to mine. "She's right, I feel it too."

By the heavy look of concern on Bethani's face, I knew something bad was about to happen. Nicolai rushed to my side protectively, while the others stared in silent anticipation.

Jeremiah's jaw muscles twitched, and I knew he was preparing himself for a fight. "What should we do?" he asked.

The ground beneath us trembled ferociously. Tree branches could be heard snapping angrily nearby.

Bethani's lavender eyes grew wide with fear. "We run!"

Suddenly hundreds of deer emerged from the edge of the forest. Their ears were tipped back, while a look of sheer terror could be seen in their big brown eyes. Their tails flicked anxiously as they bounded towards us.

"We won't have time to outrun them," I said. Letting the familiar electric current run throughout my body, I whispered, "Protection." A bright, white current escaped from my fingertips and snaked across the ground like lightning would flash across a night sky. The energy joined together in a jagged circle around us. The frightened deer, sensing the strong forces, kept their distance from our group.

"I see she's remembered her talents," Daniel called out over the loud tramping.

"Yet, she doesn't recall you," my father joked.

"She will," Daniel promised.

My eyes darted nervously to each of my companions. It was important to me that I kept them all safe. Nicolai's eyes met mine and I could see from the frown on his face he was worried. Jeremiah was right; what if I hadn't been able to keep them safe? I could've lost the one thing I had fought so hard to keep—love. My heart was suddenly full of regret.

A few more deer ran skittishly past us. Once I was sure we were out of harm's way, I dismissed the protective energy around us.

"It looks like they're en route to town," my father noted, pointing to the buildings that lay in the direction the deer were heading.

"What could possibly scare a forest animal so much that they would take their chances in the human world?" Bethani asked.

The forest beckoned to me as I stared into it. "I don't know, but we're about to find out." I took comfort in the familiar touch of Nicolai's hand on my shoulder.

"Wait." He wrapped his arms around my waist. His earthy scent sent butterflies to my stomach. "I'm sorry," he said.

I put my finger against his cool lips and whispered, "I'm sorry too." In one swift motion, he moved my finger away and pushed his lips against mine. The power ran through both of us and for a moment the world stood still. Our souls touched, reminding us that our love was special. It was meant to be.

A breathless, romantic sigh could be heard behind us. "Wow," Bethani said. "This is just like one of those Hallmark movies you watch with me, Angelina."

Stepping away from my special moment with Nicolai, I too let out my own breathless, romantic sigh. Wow was right! Nicolai pushed a stray strand of hair behind my ear lovingly. "I am yours and you are mine. I will love you forever."

"Well, if you two teenagers are done making out, do you think we can get going?" Daniel asked, emotionless.

Giving Daniel a dirty look, I pulled away from Nicolai and stared into the forest. I was really beginning to dislike this guy.

Nicolai nudged me gently. "Come on, don't let him get to you. He's harmless. You'll see."

"We'll see." The forest beckoned to me once again. Something terrible was happening deep within it. I could feel it deep in my soul. It desperately needed our help.

"It's dying," I said.

"What is?" Nicolai asked.

"The forest," I replied, knowing we were the only ones that could save it.

Chapter 15
Triple Spiral

Ctephanyi rummaged through her top dresser drawer, in search of the small wooden box bound in dried deer leather. The box had arrived on her doorstep only a few days ago, and she knew the emblem that had been burnt into the dried leather well. It was their family crest, a triple spiral with the first letters of their name intertwined. When she saw the crest, it became apparent who the gift was from: her estranged husband, Elias. She had been afraid to open it. Their final memories together in the forest had been tragic. She still wasn't quite ready to let those feelings of hurt and betrayal resurface, so she had hidden the box out of sight. As humans say, out of sight, out of mind, right?

Her fingers ran across something soft and smooth. Smiling, she pulled out the small wooden treasure and traced her finger along the edges of the triple spiral. This emblem represented the powers of maiden, mother, and crone. It was the symbol of her people and the power they possessed in growth and transition. Their family initials intertwined within the symbol brought love and light.

Suddenly the teacups that were decoratively displayed in an old, open hutch began to chatter noisily in the next room. She felt an odd tremble under her feet and slammed her dresser drawer shut. A dark, ominous feeling crept into her human soul. It was a new feeling for her, but it let her know something was very wrong.

Holding the wooden box close, she headed to the front of the house. She jumped as her teacups fell and shattered, one by one, onto the hardwood floor. She pulled open her front door and her body went numb from adrenaline. Her cold fingers loosened around the box and it slipped out of her hand. It tumbled softly down the front steps and landed on the grass a few feet away. With her hands trembling slightly, she stood in awe of the large whitetail deer that stood in front of her. She turned her head and saw hundreds more coming towards her.

"I believe this is yours," a familiar voice said.

She turned and her chin began to quiver as the familiar voice added, "You never opened it."

She couldn't take her eyes off him. "How do you know that?"

"The seal over the emblem isn't cracked," he answered.

She lowered her hand and took the tiny box from him. "I was afraid to open it."

His eyes grew curious. "*You* were afraid?"

She nodded and looked down at the small wooden treasure in her hand. "I couldn't let Nicolai down again."

"I understand."

She looked back up, her eyes brimming with human emotion. "You do?"

He took a step towards her. "We both let him down."

"Elias…" she let each syllable of his name fall from her lips slowly.

He put his hand over hers and nodded to the box. "Open it."

She pulled at the leather, breaking the emblem. Tiny gold sparks fell from its bindings. She gasped, startled by its magic. The leather fell into pieces, revealing a smooth rune-covered wooden box.

"You've been a human for far too long my dear." He laughed. "You've forgotten that our leather bindings are magical and can only be opened by who the gift is intended for."

She smiled at the familiarity of the runes that covered the box. It was like the wooden box her wedding band had come in. She ran her fingers along the top of the box and put slight pressure on the middle of it. Three spirals linked by one center appeared and glowed brightly. Counting under her breath, she whispered. "One."

"Two," Elias whispered.

"Three." There was a tiny click and the top of the box popped open. "Elias, it's beautiful!" she exclaimed, pulling out a silver necklace with a rune-covered heart pendant. In the center of the heart pendant was a picture of Nicolai, Elias, Angelina, and herself. Next to the pendant lay a small scroll tied with a thin, red satin ribbon.

"Please, before you say anything, read."

She nodded and unfolded the paper carefully. She felt her eyes begin to mist again and sniffled. "Darn these human emotions."

"They look well on you." He smiled and looked down, somewhat embarrassed.

Returning the smile, she read the simple message meant just for her:

You were right. The world around us doesn't care who you are or where you come from. All species are created equal and I would rather live amongst the humans than live without you or our child.

Please forgive me.

"I guess these human emotions really aren't that bad, are they?" she said, blinking back tears.

"I guess not," he agreed.

She picked up the necklace and handed it to him. Smiling, he walked behind her and pushed her long, red hair to the side. His hand was cool against her soft, pale skin. He latched the fragile necklace and turned her around to face him. She felt beautiful in his eyes. This was one human emotion she would always cherish. The feeling of real, wholesome, unconditional love. Not the story book, imaginary kind of love that people look for their entire lives. This was the kind of love you would die for. This was the kind of love Nicolai and Angelina had.

Nostalgia hit Ctephanyi like a ton of bricks. She finally understood. It took her to become a human being to see that true love does conquer all. It's more powerful than any one thing or creature on Earth.

"Maybe these emotions are just what we needed to bring us back together as a family," he said.

"A real family," she sighed.

"Look at the love Angelina and Nicolai have. We can't deny the love they share between them, plus"—he stared into her cobalt ice blue eyes—"she gave us a second chance at life. Angelina gave us a second chance to get it right."

Ctephanyi looked at the herd of deer that surrounded them. "Look at all of them…"

The loving look fell from his face. "My love, the Earth is dying."

Nausea filtered into Ctephanyi's body like a parasite looking for an easy host. "What do you mean, the Earth is dying? It's an everlasting factor to all that is living."

"It's dying, Ctephanyi, and the only person that can save it is Angelina."

Her light eyes widened. "I was warned, a long time ago. He was a child then. He meant nothing to us."

"What do you mean?"

"Nothing." She shrugged, holding her secrets to herself. If Elias knew, he would be disappointed, and she had already disappointed enough people. Nobody could ever know what she had witnessed. This was her chance to make it right.

Ctephanyi looked down at the pendant. Life meant so much more now than it had in the past. Now she had a reason to live. "No."

"No?" Elias questioned, curiously.

"No," she repeated. "We are going to fix what we should have fixed a long time ago."

"How?" he questioned, raising his brow.

"Hecate has restored all that was mine," she said proudly.

His face twisted into a look of awe and surprise. "With what stipulation?"

She smirked. "The stipulation was that I save Angelina from a fate that involved Tristan."

"How?" he stuttered.

"We need to stop the Crimson Moon from rising."

"So, the legends are true?" Elias asked. His eyes gave him away. She could see that he knew just how much trouble they were in.

Her hand clasped the pendant around her neck protectively. "Tristan has returned, and he's here to take what he thinks is his," she said.

Elias frowned deeply. "Well, that explains why the Earth is dying."

Now it was her turn to look confused. "What do you mean?"

"Whoever brought him back knew if he walked the Earth again, it would die a slow death. His life force poisons the Earth with every step he takes, and in every step, he grows stronger. Soon he will be unstoppable."

"We need to hurry. The crimson moss is already dying, and Tristan will be looking for Angelina, as she is the key to life." The cheap, colored contact lenses she wore couldn't hide the determination in her eyes.

"Where is Tristan hiding?" Elias asked.

"Hiding?" she scoffed. "He's not hiding, he's waiting for her to find him. He's out in the open. He's purposefully putting himself out there so she will be intrigued by his fearlessness."

"We should find her before he does, so we can enlighten her mind. She needs to be ready for the evil she is about to face." He gazed into the crimson-colored forest and frowned.

"What about the deer? The humans aren't going to understand this. They're going to be terrified."

"There's nothing we can do about the deer right now. The humans will likely blame it on the folklore that the 'mythical creatures' living in the forest did it."

"You're right, Elias."

"The deer will refuse to return to the forest as long as evil walks inside it," he said.

"I don't blame them."

"We can deal with the humans and their reaction later," Elias noted. "Right now, we have to save the Earth."

Ctephanyi laughed.

He looked at her questioningly. "What?"

"I'm sorry, but right then, you sound like one of those cheesy human superheroes on TV," she said

He laughed along with her. "These humans do have an odd fascination with super beings."

They looked at each other momentarily before laughing in unison. Folklore had deemed their species as monsters, but fiction, on the other hand, would deem superheroes.

Taking his wife by the hand, Elias smiled. "Shall we go save the Earth?"

With a smile, she nodded. "Why yes, Elias. Let's go be superheroes and save the day."

Chapter 16
The Key

The forest embraced them in silence as they made their way through the dense brush. Its peaceful nature seemed overshadowed by something dark and menacing.

Jeremiah pointed to the top of a nearby oak tree. "Look at the moss, it's dying."

He was right. The ever-intriguing vines of crimson moss that were swirled around the tree trunks had begun to turn dark and ash away.

"It has begun," my father said, his eyes shifting to the tree tops. "If the Crimson Moon rises, it will be too late."

I turned to look at him sharply. "What did you just say?"

He looked back at me curiously. "About what?"

"The moon."

"Once a keeper of the Underworld has risen to the Earth's surface, they have seven days to find the key to immortality, otherwise they are forced to return and endure another ten thousand years of death."

"Tristan is a keeper of the Underworld?"

My father nodded. "Yes, he is."

"And this key to immortality, where is it located?

The expression on his face hardened and he took a moment to gather his thoughts. He walked over and our eyes met. "Angelina, the key is you."

It took me a moment to digest what he'd said. I was the key to immortality? I felt Daniel staring at me. "I suppose you knew about this, too?"

He shoved his hands into his pockets and shifted his weight uncomfortably.

"Answer me!"

He looked down shamefully. "Yes, I knew."

"And what about you?" I asked, switching my attention to Bethani.

Her face paled. "Yes."

"How long have you known?" I asked.

"Always," she replied.

"Didn't any of you think maybe, just maybe, it would have been nice to tell me this?"

"Angelina, you wouldn't have understood," my father said.

"Mathias was right," I whispered.

"Mathias? When did you see him?" my father asked in surprise.

Nicolai took a step forward and answered for me. "He came to her in a dream."

My cheeks flushed in anger instantly. "How did you...wait, you read my mind?"

He looked away sheepishly. "You were panicking and talking in your sleep. It worried me."

"You promised you would never do that," I hissed through clenched teeth.

"We don't have time for a lover's quarrel," Daniel interrupted. His loud voice echoed around us.

Drawing in a deep breath, I pushed past Nicolai. "How long do we have before the Crimson Moon rises?"

"Three days," my father replied.

"Well then, we best get going," I replied. I whistled and motioned for Snow to follow me. She trotted along behind me, growling softly as she passed by Nicolai.

"Yeah, I know," Nicolai muttered under his breath.

"She's not growling at you," Bethani said, reaching for her bow. "She's growling at the two people that are coming up behind you."

Nicolai's fiery orange eyes lit up as he turned around. "It can't be."

"Why is *he* with her? Is this some sort of sick joke?" I asked.

Ctephanyi and Elias were together again. They looked cool and calm as they made their way toward us.

Jeremiah puffed out his manly chest. "Don't worry, we got this," he promised.

"There's nothing to fear from Elias," Ctephanyi called out.

Elias smiled. "I think you've forgotten your mother has spectacular hearing."

Snow's growl deepened and she snarled as they walked passed her.

Ctephanyi bent down and held her hand out to the wolf pup. "Angelina, what are you feeding this animal? She looks as if she's grown three sizes since I last saw her."

Snow sniffed at Ctephanyi's long dress. Sensing familiarity, her growl immediately disappeared and she began to wag her tail happily. "This wolf pup here is pretty special," she said, her icy white eyes twinkled with mischief.

"You don't happen to know what she's talking about, do you?" I asked Jeremiah.

He looked at me and kicked at the grass. "Maybe..."

Now my curiosity was piqued. "Where did you get Snow?"

"A beautiful woman in a long, golden laced robe came to me. She told me the pup would help with your loss of Cole."

"A woman in a golden laced robe gave her to you to give to me?"

He nodded. "One afternoon, I was chopping wood and she just appeared out of nowhere. She said it broke her heart to see you so sad."

"What did she look like?" I asked.

"I don't know," he muttered. "She was beautiful and wearing a robe."

"That's helpful," I replied.

Ctephanyi ran her hand down Snow's smooth, white fur and looked up. "It was your mother, Angelina."

"My mother? She's not allowed to come back, or so I thought."

She stood up and dusted herself off. "She can't. She broke the rules."

"Like mother, like daughter." Daniel scoffed.

"You always have something cocky to say, don't you?" I asked, giving Daniel a dirty look. "Ctephanyi, can you tell me what's so special about Snow?"

"If what you're asking is if this animal is Cole reborn, then no, it's not." She smiled. "She was simply made for you."

"What does that mean?" I asked confused.

"In about two days, she will be full grown. Though her teeth are sharp like razors, they are poisonous also. One nip could potentially kill you."

Bending down, I hugged my white furry friend.

"She was made to love you, Angelina. Your mother took some of her love and put it into this little white beast."

I sucked in my breath and tried to maintain my composure. "What a truly thoughtful gift."

"Just because she can't be here with you on Earth, doesn't mean she can't take care of you from up above," my father said. His expression was full of love and admiration.

Clearing my throat, I picked up Snow and hugged her tight. "Yeah, I guess you're right."

He put his arm around me and squeezed. "We should get going."

Snow licked his face. Apparently, she had been made to love him also.

"Lovely." He laughed. "Poisonous puppy breath."

I set Snow back down on the ground and admired her beauty. Ctephanyi was right, she had grown had least three sizes. I had been so wound up in everything that had been going on that I hadn't even noticed. It was hard to believe she would be full grown two days from now. She was going to be beautiful and deadly.

Walking past Nicolai, I gave him a quick nudge and smirked. "You better not make her mad." As if she could understand me, she looked up at Nicolai and let out a short growl.

He shook his head. "Funny."

Snow snarled again and bared her sharp teeth.

He raised his hands in protest. "Okay, I get it," he muttered.

I laughed.

"Oh, so now you're coming at me, too?" he joked. "I can't win." Grabbing my hand, he pulled me a step closer to him. Instead of pulling away, I took another step forward. Smiling, we kissed each other.

"Ready?" he asked.

"Yes, sir." I replied.

Side by side, the three of us headed deeper into the forest. We were an unstoppable team. Tristan stood no chance—at least that's what I kept telling myself.

Chapter 17
Bad Dreams

We walked until dusk and then decided it was best to find a suitable place to set up camp. According to Daniel, we were only about half a day behind Tristan. I was curious how he knew that, but I didn't like him enough to ask.

I threw a stick at Jeremiah. "Are you going to start that fire or what?"

He shrugged and threw the stick back at me. "What?"

I rolled my eyes. "Funny."

"Funny looking, maybe," my father joked.

We all laughed and settled in to our makeshift campsite. We had traveled light, so we had to use what survival skills we knew. Nicolai was assigned food duty, while Daniel assigned himself to do nothing more than doze off against a tree. Snow curled up against my legs, snoring lightly. Jeremiah worked on building his "manly" fire, while my father lay on the ground and stared up at the stars that poked through the treetops. I imagined he was probably thinking about my mother.

"Hey, Angelina."

"Yeah, Jeremiah?"

"Do you really think we'll be able to stop him?"

Giving myself a moment to think, I answered simply. "Yes."

He flung a twig into the bright, blazing fire. "How can you be so sure?" he asked.

"Well." I pointed at the stars over our heads. "We won't allow ourselves to fail. There are too many people up there we would disappoint."

He continued throwing twigs and dried up moss bits into the fire. "What did Mathias tell you in your dream?"

Looking down at the bundle of white fur snuggled against my legs, I sighed. "He said I would have to make a choice."

"What kind of choice?"

"One that will save the world," I said.

"You can't tell me?" he asked.

My eyes had begun to get heavy as the day had finally taken its toll on me. Scooting down, I used Snow as a warm pillow. "No, Jeremiah," I said. "I *won't* tell you."

* * *

Smoke billowed out of the broken windows of the bed and breakfast. A faint cry for help could be heard from inside the burning structure as the flames licked the air. I looked around for help, but I was utterly alone. Taking a deep breath, I barged through the old worn door and threw my arms up to shield my face from the ash and smoke. I heard the cry again and made my way up the stairs, avoiding the hot flames that tried to kiss my delicate skin.

"Please," the voice sobbed. "Help me."

"Hello?" I called out. "Where are you?"

"Please," the voice moaned. "Someone help me."

The thick smoke filled my lungs. Coughing, I covered my mouth. "I'm coming," I promised. Realizing the voice was coming from my room, I rushed down the hallway as quickly as I could. Once I reached the bedroom door, I immediately grabbed the doorknob and screamed out in pain. The hot metal seared the skin right off the palm of hand.

"I'm in here!" the voice called out. "Please hurry!"

The dark smoke was overwhelming. "I've had just about enough of this," I coughed. Sparks of electricity vibrated throughout my body. "Life be still."

I opened my eyes, and to my surprise, everything around me had frozen in place. Time had temporarily stopped. I pulled my shirt up over my head and thanked myself for remembering to wear a tank top underneath it. Balling up the shirt, I used it to turn the doorknob safely; however, it still refused to open. I threw my weight up against it, and it finally flung open.

"Help me," the small voice begged.

A tear fell down my cheek once I realized who the small voice belonged to. It was me, as a child. "Don't be afraid," I smiled. Using my unscathed, dirty hand, I wiped the tears from my face.

She looked at me, fearful. "He's coming for me."

"Who, sweetie? Who's coming for you?"

"Death."

Feeling the heat on my skin once again, I knew the hands of time had begun to tick. I held my hand out to her, and she reached for it. I smiled at her reassuringly to let her know I was there to help. Suddenly, she pulled back and hid her face in her hands.

A chill ran through my body and I turned around. Emerald-green eyes greeted me and I knew I was too late. The bedroom door slammed shut and I screamed.

Nicolai's strong hands shook me by the shoulders. "Angelina, wake up!"

Snow barked loudly in my ear, and my eyes flew open. "Where is she?" I asked, looking around the campsite frantically.

"Who?" Jeremiah asked, a wild look in his eyes.

My father looked to Daniel for help. "Honey, calm down," my father urged.

I looked around frantically. "Where is the child?"

"Angelina, there's no one else here," Nicolai answered.

"Then how do you explain this?"

My father took a step back and looked at my hand in horror. "Angelina, how did you burn yourself?"

"He's entering her dreams," Daniel replied.

Nicolai's eyes burned brightly. "How is that even possible?"

He smirked. "Jealous he can do that and you can't?"

My father looked at him sternly. "Daniel…"

"Fine," he muttered. "The child in her dream is manifestation of her innocence, and he's trying to take it away from her."

"Why would he do that?" Jeremiah questioned.

"Because if he can take away her innocence then he can take away her soul," he said.

Nicolai took my hand into his and gently kissed the burn. "I won't let him get to you," he promised.

Flinching from the pain, I pulled my hand away from him quickly. "He already has."

"Calm down, child," Ctephanyi said. She wrapped her arms around me protectively. "Angelina, your soul is your own, and he cannot take it unless you let him."

I buried my head in her chest. "I won't let him have it…I can't."

She caressed my hair softly and whispered. "You are more powerful than you know, dear. Unlock the hidden doors in your mind, and you will unlock the power to defeat him."

I shook my head and sobbed, "We don't have enough time. What if I fail?"

She pulled away and grabbed me firmly by the shoulders. "Angelina, look at me."

It was hard to avoid her icy white eyes.

"Do not be afraid. You are the deadliest creature on the face of this planet. It is he who should fear you."

Ctephanyi continued. "You left this Earth once and came back stronger to keep this world intact. You are here to protect humanity. That, my child, is your destiny."

Maybe she was right. Everything, regardless of how terrible it had been, had happened for a reason. *I* had been put here to protect humanity. *I* had died to save humans from killing themselves and had come back to protect them once again. This was *my* destiny. This was my soul, and he wasn't going to get it, or me.

Chapter 18
Betrayal

Tristan took a step back and let out a frustrated yell, "She will be mine!" He fell to his knees and pounded the dew-drenched ground with his fist. "I must have her soul!"

"What can I do?" A sweet voice asked calmly.

He looked up at her with wild eyes. "Bring her to me."

She nodded. "Our deal still stands?"

"You bring me Angelina, and yes, I will honor our arrangement."

She smiled wickedly. "Then I shall do as you ask."

"Then go," he waved her on, "but remember one thing."

She nodded. "Yes?"

"Do not disappoint me," he warned.

"Disappointment is only failure for the weak," she said, "and I am not weak."

He smirked. "We shall see." He watched her disappear into the woods and sighed. He didn't have much time left and Angelina was the key to his salvation from the hell he had been sentenced to. He loved her and vowed to make her love him in return. He would own her soul for all of eternity and together they would rule the world.

A gruff voice interrupted his thoughts. "Master?"

"What could you possibly want?" he asked, annoyed by the distraction.

"We have a problem."

Tristan cocked his head to the side and groaned in displeasure. "What could possibly be wrong now?"

Mathias lowered his head in shame. "She's acquired two more people in her party."

Tristan took a step towards him, causing the man to fall to his knees and beg for mercy. "Please, master, I was unaware of this until just now."

"Who are these two new additions?" He hissed.

Mathias' voice trembled. "Elias."

"And?"

"Ctephanyi," he said. Mathias grabbed at Tristan's feet. "Please, have mercy on me."

Tristan kicked his hands away. "Ctephanyi?! How could you possibly miss such a pertinent piece of information?" he bellowed.

"Hecate hid it from me."

"Hecate," he snarled angrily.

"She returned Ctephanyi's powers."

Tristan took another step forward and backhanded his hooded henchman, sending him sprawling across the ground. "You idiot!"

"Please," he begged, "It won't happen again."

"You're right." Tristan laughed wickedly. "It won't happen again." He hit him again.

Mathias struggled to lift his head. "Please…"

Tristan reached down and pulled the hood off of Mathias' head. "How do you think your dear Angelina would feel if I sent a little birdie her way with some pertinent information about you?"

"You wouldn't."

He took a step back and smirked. "Are you so sure?"

They stared at each other momentarily before Tristan threw the hood on the ground. "She'll find out soon enough."

The man reached for the hood and suddenly found his hand crushed under Tristan's boot. "Tell me, Mathias, what does the future hold?"

Mathias looked up at him, his eyes running through a multitude of colors. "The future has not yet been written, Tristan. Only Angelina knows what's in store for it."

"How about your future?" he asked, "what does it hold for you?"

Mathias winced in pain as Tristan ground his foot into his hand. "My future holds much more than yours does," he answered, his eyes turning to their blood-red color.

Tristan let out a hearty laugh. "Is that so?"

Mathias nodded and smirked. "Angelina will understand."

Tristan crouched down and grabbed Mathias by the hair, pulling him closer. "She will banish you for your betrayal. She will cut your tongue out and remove your unique eyes."

Mathias glared at him, pure hate emanating from his soul. "Tristan, you shall never have her. She knows of the task that has been set before her and she will not fail."

A look of surprise crossed his face. "You little sneak."

Mathias braced himself for the blow. It came swift and it came hard. He went rolling across the ground like a ragdoll. He used what strength he had left and pulled himself into a sitting position against a nearby tree. "Kill me if you must. You may be my master, but you do not own my soul, and she will never give you hers."

Tristan stood up and dusted himself off. "My dear Mathias, I'm not going to kill you."

Mathias eyed him up suspiciously.

"I'm going to let her do it," he retorted. He kicked the black hood towards him. "I'm going to let her rip the soul out of your weak body and feed your remains to the wolves."

"We shall see." Mathias smirked. "The future is in her hands, not in yours."

Chapter 19
Sins

Nicolai stroked Angelina's long, wild hair—pushing strands of it away from her face while she slept soundly next to him. He was curious what she was dreaming about. He had promised her he would stay out of her mind. He'd already broken that promise once and wasn't about to break it again. He was so worried about her. Things had been different between them lately. She seemed constantly on edge, unbalanced by something she had seen in her first nightmare. Though he'd regretted peeking into her mind, he had seen it too. Regardless of what decisions she would have to make, he would stand by her.

She smiled subconsciously, and he smiled right along with her. He figured she was at least dreaming of something pleasant with that sweet little smile that graced her adorable face. He caressed her cheek lovingly and thought of how far they'd come. Their love had passed through the boundaries of life and death itself to come together so they could be one. No matter what conflicts they faced, he knew they would always strive to overcome them. They were a team, and with their love guiding them, they would be unstoppable.

Looking up into the night sky, he could see Angelina's earthly mother and Hecate watching over her protectively from above. They both loved her with such fierceness that he pitied Tristan's fate. Angelina had so much love on her side. If she could only see it all...

He sighed and caught Daniel staring at her.

"When are you going to tell her?" Nicolai questioned.

Startled, Daniel blinked and looked away.

"She will figure it out soon enough you know," Nicolai noted.

"Figure out what?" Jeremiah asked mid yawn.

"Nothing," Daniel mumbled under his breath.

Jeremiah stood up and stretched. "It doesn't sound like nothing."

"He's afraid she won't accept him," Bethani's sweet voice chimed in.

Jeremiah looked from Daniel to Bethani curiously. "Accept him?"

She smiled sweetly and nodded. "For his sins."

"Shut up," Daniel ordered angrily.

Ctephanyi's voice rang out of the darkness behind them. "Do not talk to her like that."

Daniel sat up a little straighter and cleared his throat. "This is none of your business."

"It becomes my business when you treat a Lady of the Forest as you are treating her, young man," she retorted.

He was speechless for a moment and then turned to face Bethani with a humble expression on his face. "I'm sorry."

She gave him her sweetest smile. "Daniel, sometimes life graces us with a decision that, regardless of our thought process, we must follow through with."

"What are you talking about?" he asked gruffly.

Bethani's light lavender eyes darkened. "Your sister will have to make the hardest decision that she will ever be faced with and you must be there for her when she does or the blood moon will rise."

The camp grew eerily quiet as they all stared at her in surprise. Finally, Angelina's father, who had been watching silently from beside the fire stood up and went to Daniel's side, "She's right, Daniel."

Daniel looked down, his hard demeanor momentarily fading. "I can't change the past."

He put his hand on Daniel's shoulder and squeezed. "She'll understand, son. Your sister will remember you for your strength, not for your weakness."

Nicolai caressed Angelina's cheek again delicately. "Listen to your father, Daniel. She doesn't remember you yet. Her mind is still too fragile for those memories to come back."

"Wait," Jeremiah said. "You're Angelina's brother?"

Daniel looked up and studied Jeremiah before answering, "Her twin brother to be exact."

Jeremiah's eyes widened at his omission. "Twin? How…but…wait…" He struggled to find the words but nothing that came out sounded right.

Ctephanyi walked over and sat down next to him. "Daniel, it is imperative that you wait until the very last moment before her decision to tell her who you are."

Elias sat down next to his wife and put his arm around her shoulder protectively. "Heed her words wisely, Daniel. Any sooner and you will cause an inexplicable amount of damage to her thought process."

"Wait a minute," Jeremiah demanded. "Someone please explain this to the 'normal' people in the group who have absolutely no idea what you're talking about."

Angelina's father chuckled and returned to his seat by the fire. "Jeremiah, your mind is just as fragile as Angelina's. I'm not so sure you could handle all the mysteries our family history hides from you."

Jeremiah glared at him. "Try me."

He sighed. "Daniel, do you want to tell the story or do you want me to?"

Daniel shrugged. "It doesn't matter. It's just as painful hearing it the fifteenth time as it is hearing it the first."

Nicolai lay his hand on the top of Angelina's head so he could sense when she was getting ready to wake up. He didn't want her to wake up in the middle of the story and hear something she wasn't ready to hear. "I will tell it."

Daniel looked up at Nicolai, surprised. "You'll tell it?"

"After all, it did involve me."

Jeremiah rolled his eyes. "Surprise."

Ctephanyi shifted her gaze towards him. "Jeremiah, some things in life must happen for other possibilities to present themselves."

He rolled his eyes again. "Well, what is the possibility of hearing this story before she wakes up?" he asked, pointing towards Angelina.

Daniel shifted his weight uneasily. "Just get it over with."

Nicolai nodded. "Fine, here we go."

Chapter 20
Memories

Recalling the past was hard, but even though his memories were bittersweet, they were his. He recalled watching his twin sister with admiration as they grew up. She had seemed so innocent with her wide, chestnut-colored eyes. She was feisty and fearless. Though she was young, his mother had told him of what a great person she was to be in the future. He had been proud to stand by her side and keep her safe.

There was one memory that stuck out more than any other.

Angelina wrinkled up her freckled nose and stuck her tongue out. "What are you looking at?"

"Do you know what they say about making faces at people?" he asked.

"No, what do they say?" She made another face at him before shoving him playfully.

He grabbed her by the side and began to tickle her feverishly. "They say your face will end up sticking that way."

She laughed uncontrollably, pushing his hands away from her. "Stop it, Daniel!" she begged.

"What are you two doing?" their father asked, stepping out of the small log cabin that was tucked away deep within the woods.

They both looked up at him innocently and together answered, "Nothing."

He gave them a stern, playful look. "Is that so?"

They looked at each other with wicked smiles upon their young, beautiful faces and nodded.

He shook his head. "You two…I don't know what I'm going to do with you." He laughed, pulling them both in for a hug.

"Father, when is Momma coming to visit us?" Angelina asked hesitantly.

He put a finger to his chin and looked at her thoughtfully. "Hmm, I don't know," he replied. He turned toward the forest and pointed. "Surprise!" he yelled.

Her gaze followed his and she let out a shrill scream. "Momma!"

Angelina skipped toward her mother in excitement.

"Daniel, aren't you going to go see your mother?" his father questioned, looking down at him.

He stared at his mother and Angelina. "I guess." He shrugged.

"Now Daniel, she loves you too, you know."

"Does she?" he asked snidely.

His father looked up at his beautiful wife and remained silent. Daniel knew the answer. Angelina was the special one. She had been born with unimaginable power that would someday save the world. He knew his mother favored her and he was okay with that. While he lived with his grandmother, it simply meant another protector for his beloved sister.

"Daniel."

"Hecate."

She frowned, "Please do not call me that. I am your mother."

Daniel shoved his hands into his pockets and kicked at the grass. "Mother," he muttered.

Angelina grabbed their mother's hand and pulled her towards them. "Mother, Daniel taught me how to climb trees today!" she exclaimed excitedly.

Their mother put her delicate hands on her hips. There was a hint of disapproval in her voice. "Is that so?" she asked.

"Yes, and then we skipped rocks in the river and chased the wolves through the forest."

"You did what?" she looked at her in shock.

"Momma, you should have seen them run! They're so fast!"

"Daniel," their mother interrupted. "How could you take her to chase…wolves?"

"We're not children anymore, Mother," he grumbled, refusing to look at her.

"Yes, you are," she scolded. "She could've been hurt, or worse, killed."

Finally, he looked up at her. "We're twelve, Mother, we're not children. As for Angelina getting hurt, do you really think with the powers she possesses she would allow anything to hurt her?"

She opened to her mouth to say something, but their father stepped between them. "Why don't we go inside for dinner?" he offered.

She cleared her throat. "That sounds lovely."

"No." Angelina's voice trembled.

Daniel looked at her and his heart stopped. He knew something was wrong. He felt a shiver run down his spine and looked behind him.

Their mother's eyes darted from him to her to the forest behind them. "Get them out of here."

"What is it?" their father asked cautiously.

"Do as I said," she ordered. "Get them out of here now—go!"

He ushered them towards the trail in front of them.

Angelina pulled at her mother's hand. "Momma, come with us."

Their mother looked at her and smiled. "Angelina, you must go with your father and brother. They will protect you."

"No, I'm not leaving without you." She stood her ground, a tear falling down her cheek in defiance.

Daniel watched the look of helplessness wash over his mother's face. At that very moment, he had the feeling this was the last time he would ever see her. "Come on, Angelina, we have to go."

She pulled her hand free of Angelina's and ushered her towards their father. "Josiah, take them and go."

"Momma, no!" she screamed, pushing her father away.

Daniel wrapped his strong arms around her waist and picked up her. She kicked at his legs and clawed at his arms. "Let me go, Daniel, let me go! I can protect her!" she protested loudly, tears streaming down her face.

A tear ran down their mother's beautiful face as she watched them flee down the trail. She turned and faced the force that came at her from within the forest. It was her ancient enemy, Tristan. He had come for her daughter and she would not allow him to have her.

"Hecate," he hissed.

"Tristan," she nodded.

"Where is she?"

"I don't know what you're talking about," she answered nonchalantly.

"Don't play games with me," he demanded.

"Who's playing games?" she scoffed, glaring at him with hatred in her eyes.

"She will be mine."

She raised her hand to the blue sky and it began to fill with dark, ominous clouds. "Over my dead body."

He held up a rune-covered amulet. It dangled lazily from its long silver rope. "If that's what it takes," he said.

She lowered her hand slowly and the dark clouds disappeared. "Where did you get that?"

He smiled at her wickedly. "My father sends his regards."

"What have you done, Tristan?"

"One way or another, she will be mine." He grinned, placing the amulet over his head. One by one the runes began to glow bright blue. "You know, funny thing about humans." He glared at her, wicked pleasure in his emerald-green eyes. "Their minds are fragile enough that any idea can be implanted into them."

"Tristan, no!" Hecate yelled lunging towards him.

The last rune lit up and time stood still. Tristan grinned, walking towards her still body. "Your daughter is such an amazing girl, isn't she?" He bent down and put his ear near her. "What's that, you say? Oh, I'm sorry, time does funny things to people, doesn't it?" He stood up and muttered, "even people like you."

"Let her go," a voice called out from behind him.

He turned around, surprised. "Well, well, where do you come from, old friend?"

"I wouldn't quite say we're friends, Tristan," she replied, her icy white eyes glowing with hate.

"You look good, Ctephanyi. Apparently, time has no effect on you. You look younger than ever."

"Time is forgiving to those who don't age."

He pointed to Hecate. "Look at her. She's an immortal. She will never age, never get a wrinkle, and always watch the ones she loves die. Aren't you jealous of that, old friend?"

"Ahh, that's where you're wrong," Ctephanyi smirked. "When Hecate walks the Earth, she ages just as the humans do."

"Maybe I should feel lucky she can't hear us or help you right now," he scoffed.

"I will not let you harm them," she replied.

He touched one of the runes and closed his eyes. "None of you matter. Only Angelina matters."

"I wouldn't do that if I were you," she warned.

He ignored her. "They will see her as a weapon of mass destruction."

"I'm going to give you one last opportunity to stop," she threatened.

"They will murder all that stand in their way. They will hunt all that are unlike them."

She shook her head and motioned to the brush behind him. "Now."

An arrow whizzed past the side of his head, grazing his ear. "If she dies during this time, her family may not meddle with her memories and her mother may not return to Earth to be with her," he continued.

The woman snarled. "How could you?"

He heard someone rush up behind him and opened his eyes. "It's too late." He winced at the pain as the sharp blade ran through him. Falling to his knees, he laughed. "You're too late."

She raised her hand, and the crimson moss snaked along the ground toward him. "You will never have her."

He looked at the young man next to her—it was Nicolai. His fiery orange eyes were filled with fear and hatred. "You love her, don't you?" Tristan asked.

The woman's icy eyes filled with surprise and she looked down at him. "You love her?"

Nicolai nodded. "My heart knows what it wants, and it wants her."

Tristan laughed and blood spewed out of his mouth. "You are fools! You can't save her."

The woman's hand rose in the air and the moss rose with it. "Tristan, do you want to know what's so similar about you and humans?"

He cocked his head to the side and smiled. "What's that?"

"You can both be killed off so damn easily." She smirked, motioning the moss to attack her target. It darted into him with such a force his body flew into the tree behind him. Tristan howled in pain. The woman took her free hand and turned Nicolai's face away from the horror in front of him. "If Angelina is the one you love, then you will be forced to protect her because I refuse. She is the daughter of Hecate, and more powerful than you could ever imagine."

He cringed as the moss tore through Tristan's muscular body. It wrapped itself around him, covering his mouth so his cries could no longer be heard.

"Mother, please…"

"Please what?" she asked. "The damage has already been done. He's implanted the seed of the desire for power into the humans. They will come for us and her."

"What about her, mother?" he asked pointing the beautiful woman that stood still in front of him.

"That, Nicolai, is the goddess Hecate."

His eyes widened. "Hecate?" he whispered.

"Yes, now we must go before time catches up," she ordered, ushering him into the forest.

He followed her, turning around and stopping briefly as he thought he caught a glimpse of another boy his age watching intently from the brush in the distance.

"Why are you stopping?" Ctephanyi asked.

"Nothing, I thought…"

"You thought what?" she asked, curiously following his gaze.

He shook his head and continued walking. "Nothing. It was nothing."

She stared momentarily at the brush and smiled. "You're right, it is nothing."

They disappeared into the forest, the crimson moss hiding their footsteps behind them, but the damage had already been done. The seed had been planted and the humans had their goal—find and control anything unlike them. Power and hate spread through them like a virus, bringing death and destruction in its wake. Species suffered at the hands of the humans and became slaves, while Tristan bided his time in the depths of the Underworld, waiting for the perfect opportunity to come back and finish what he'd started—and that time was now.

Chapter 21
Choices

Jeremiah stared in awe at Ctephanyi. "Well, just damn," he exclaimed. "It all kind of makes sense now, except one thing…"

Nicolai looked up at him questioningly.

"What happened to Daniel?"

Nicolai lowered his eyes. "Ah, good question. Let's let him finish his story."

Jeremiah's eyes darted to Daniel who was still leaning up against the tree—a smug look on his chiseled face. He sighed and rolled his eyes. "I suppose I can finish. You aren't going to leave me alone until I do."

"Is she still asleep?" Josiah asked, motioning to Angelina.

Nicolai smiled. "Yes, she's dreaming."

Daniel took a deep breath and frowned. "Basically, my dad over there had met up with Nicolai's mother when we were younger. I had been staying with my grandmother when that took place. Though I thought of her often, I worried for her safety, so I left her alone, until the day she sought *me* out."

Ctephanyi's eyebrows rose in question. "What do you mean?"

He shrugged. "It doesn't matter. I wasn't the important one."

A look of hurt washed over Josiah's face. "That's not true, Daniel."

Daniel looked up at him. "It was the truth. Angelina was the one that needed protection. Hey, I was okay with it. I just don't understand why you wouldn't let me help protect her, too."

His father's voice grew defensive. "Daniel, you were so young."

"I was old enough to know that I loved my sister more than anything in this world," he retorted angrily. "She was my twin. Every single feeling she ever felt, I felt. All the fear, hatred, sadness…I felt it all and I couldn't be there for her."

Jeremiah watched them bicker back and forth and suddenly understood, "You were separated. That's why she doesn't remember you."

Daniel shifted his gaze towards him, anger set deep within his eyes. "I was there the day it mattered."

His father narrowed his eyes. "What day?"

"The day she died," he answered, his nose slightly flaring. "I killed her."

Nicolai's eyes flashed, fire filling them instantly. "What did you just say?"

Ctephanyi put her hand on her sons' shoulder, "Listen."

"That's right." His voice filled with weakness. "I killed her."

"But why?" Jeremiah asked, shocked by Daniel's admission.

He shook his head and stared into the fire. "Because she asked me to, that's why."

His father stared at him. "Why would she do that?"

"Because she was the strong one, father. She wanted to save humanity, so she did what she had to."

"The men that took advantage of her in the woods…" Nicolai hissed.

"I planned it," Daniel admitted.

"They tortured her," Nicolai said through clenched teeth.

"No, my dear Nicolai." He shook his head. "I was the one that ran the blade through her fragile body. I was the one who pretended to chastise her in front of those men."

Nicolai stared at him and fought the urge to rip him apart. "I found her."

"I know."

"You were there."

"Yes."

"How could you do it? Your own sister!" He pushed his mother's hand away from him. Snow opened her eyes.

"Keep your voice down, you're going to wake her."

Snow licked Angelina's hand and she stirred slightly. Nicolai lowered his voice. "You murdered your own sister."

Daniel stood up and Jeremiah followed suit, stepping in between him and Nicolai.

"Do you know what it's like to have to kill the one thing that means the most to you? She was my world, Nicolai," he growled. "When she died, I lost a piece of my soul. I lost the only thing I ever cared about. Do you know how that feels, tell me…do you know how that feels?!"

Angelina's eyes fluttered open and she sat up groggily, pulling away from Nicolai. "What's going on?"

"I know exactly what that feels like, Daniel." He looked over at Angelina's puzzled face. "She died in my arms. I was there the moment she took her last breath."

Daniel spun around and punched the tree in front of him. "None of you will understand the emptiness I've felt after losing her. I loved her and did as she wanted. That's all that matters. I don't give a shit what any of you think." He punched the tree, leaving his own blood on the busted bark before storming off into the forest.

"Daniel!" Josiah called out after him.

Ctephanyi put her hand on his shoulder. "Let him go."

"But…"

Elias cleared his throat. "She's right. Let him come to terms with his anger."

Josiah sat down next to his daughter and gave her a weak smile. She returned his smile and leaned into his loving arms.

"I'm sorry," he said.

Confusion ran through her beautiful face as she looked at each one of them. He knew she would eventually find out the truth and when she did, he wondered what would happen. Everything made sense now.

He glanced up at the tree and studied the broken bark. There were traces of Daniel's blood, but there was also something else. "No way…" he whispered, walking over to the tree. He ran his hand over the fresh moss feeding off his blood.

"What is that?" Ctephanyi questioned, her icy eyes watching him intently.

"The moss, look at it."

The mossy tendril soaked the blood up like a sponge. It pulsed bright red as it continued to feed off the bloody mess.

"It's feeding off his blood," Jeremiah said.

Fiery anger was still visible in his orange eyes. "What does that mean?" Nicolai asked.

"My dear son." Ctephanyi frowned. "It means we're running out of time."

Bethani's lavender eyes flickered with worry. "If the moss were to reach the humans…"

"They'll all die," Elias finished.

Jeremiah pulled his hand away from the moss protectively. "What do you mean they'll all die?"

Angelina picked up Snow and held her close. She watched quietly from the safety of her father's strong arms.

"The crimson moss is a living thing and when a soulless creature walks the Earth, the moss stops feeding off the Earth because of the poison that fills it."

Elias patted Ctephanyi's leg lovingly. "So, it starts looking for something healthy, something fresh and alive…"

"Like a human?" Jeremiah's mouth dropped open.

"Like a human," Ctephanyi said.

"Are you telling me that if we don't stop this Tristan guy, the moss is going to start attacking people?"

"That's exactly what I'm saying." She looked up at the moon. "When the moon is full of blood, the Earth will die."

"What?" he asked stunned.

"If the Crimson Moon rises, we will be too late."

Jeremiah stared into the fire, unable to speak. He couldn't imagine the people of his hometown being torn apart by the moss that had intrigued so many people throughout the world. It had always been harmless, or so he had thought until now.

Chapter 22
Blood Hunger

I stared at all of them, astonished by the fiasco I had awoken to. I put Snow down gently and she huffed in disappointment. I smiled and touched her cold, wet nose lightly with my finger. "Don't you huff at me, little girl." She licked my finger and trotted over to Ctephanyi, who caressed her silky fur. I stood up and went to Jeremiah, who was still studying the mysterious blood-eating moss.

"Look at that." He pointed, completely astonished by what he was seeing. "It's feeding off his blood."

"And it's growing," I noted.

His eyes widened. "It is!"

I reached up to touch it and he stopped me. "Angelina, don't touch it."

My intuition began to take over and this time I was going to trust it. "I can do this," I whispered. I nodded touched the soft moss gently. It wound itself around my finger and ran up my arm.

"Angelina!" Jeremiah stumbled backwards in horror.

I looked up and smiled. "It's okay, it doesn't hurt."

Ctephanyi laughed. "She is one with the moss, Jeremiah. It's not going to eat her."

"What?" he asked, horrified by the sight in front of him.

"She controls all living things, the moss being one of them." Nicolai laughed.

"Are you telling me she can stop it from eating people?"

Nicolai laughed again. "That's exactly what I'm saying."

Jeremiah felt his heart begin to calm itself. "So it won't destroy our town?"

The smile fell from Nicolai's face. "Well...I didn't say that."

Jeremiah stared at him, confused by his statement.

"You see, she can control the moss, but if Tristan takes her soul..."

"She'll use the moss to destroy the town," he realized.

"Exactly."

"Well, I suppose we shouldn't let that happen now should we." I said.

"Precisely," Ctephanyi said, chiming in.

"Should we go get Daniel?" I asked.

My father looked up at me, sadness filling his eyes. "Perhaps you should go get him."

Confused, I stared at them. "Okay, but he doesn't like me all that much…"

Elias chuckled, and Ctephanyi followed suit.

"I'll go with you," Nicolai offered.

"No, I'll be alright."

He stood up, and in a flash, I found myself against his cool chest. I breathed him in and the butterflies returned. "Nicolai…"

He put his finger against my lips. "Angelina, time is against us and I need you to know that regardless of whatever happens, I will always love you."

I looked up at him and tried to read his facial expression. "I…"

"No, I need you to listen to me. I love you and I want you to be mine. Forever."

I nodded, still confused.

Nicolai looked at his mother. "Will you do it?"

Her eyes lit up. "It would be an honor."

My father looked at us. "Now, you all just wait a minute," he said, standing up, "this should be her choice, too."

I stared into Nicolai's beautiful eyes and suddenly knew what he meant. "Nicolai…I…"

"No." Daniel's voice boomed over us. "I will not allow this to happen."

I spun around to face him. "Who the hell are you to try and tell me what I can and can't do?"

My father rushed to my side. "He's just angry, Angelina, pay him no attention."

"Daniel, what's your deal?" I asked, taking a step towards him.

He took another step towards me. "I can't let you do this."

I turned to Ctephanyi. "Do it."

She stood up and took a step towards us, stopping as Daniel pulled out his knife. "No, Angelina, I can't allow this to happen."

Electricity shot through my body. "Daniel, I'm warning you…step back or else."

He took another step forward. "Angelina, don't do this. Marrying into his family is a mistake. No good has ever come from *their* kind."

Everything moved in slow motion. Nicolai pushed past me and Jeremiah jumped in between them. My hand rose and the crimson moss darted across the ground and wound itself tightly around Daniel's legs, pulling him towards a nearby oak tree. My father jumped up and came towards us. I lifted my other hand and without thinking, sent out an invisible force that flung him across the ground.

"Angelina!" Jeremiah yelled out, fear in his eyes. "Stop!"

It was too late. I took a step towards Daniel and motioned for his knife to come to me. It flew across the ground and found its way to my hand. "I'm sick and tired of you being an issue."

"Angelina, no!" Nicolai reached around me and I thrust the knife through his hand and into Daniel's shoulder.

I fell to the ground as an immense pain ran through my shoulder. "What the heck?"

The moss fell to the ground and Daniel yanked the knife out of it. "Angelina!" he cried out, falling to the ground beside me.

"Why am I bleeding?" I asked.

"Because we are one," he answered, blood pouring out of his wound.

I turned to look at Nicolai. He was holding his hand, hurt in his ember eyes. "I'm so sorry."

"Angelina, look at me," Daniel ordered.

I felt weak and dizzy. "I…I'm sorry."

"Shh, it's okay," he said, pulling me close to him. He stroked my hair and I closed my eyes, "Angelina, I'm the one that's sorry."

"For what?" I whispered.

"I shouldn't have listened to you," his voice cracked. "I shouldn't have done it."

"Done what?" I asked, darkness taking ahold of me.

"I've regretted it every day since. I'm so sorry." A tear fell down his cheek and I felt it kiss my forehead.

"Daniel…"

"Yes?"

"Who are you?"

He kissed my forehead and rocked back and forth me with me in his arms. I let the darkness take ahold of me and passed out.

Chapter 23
Safe

Nicolai rushed to Angelina's side. "Is she okay?!"

Ctephanyi was next to us in a flash. "Her human body is in shock."

"From what?" Jeremiah asked, worry in his voice.

Snow whimpered from behind Elias' legs.

"When she hit Daniel, their souls reconnected."

Jeremiah looked at her, confused. "I thought they were twins, weren't their souls already connected?"

"No, she was reborn, remember?" Nicolai reminded him.

"Now what will happen?" Jeremiah asked.

"I...don't know. I've never seen this happen before."

"How do you feel, Daniel?" Josiah questioned.

"Let me stab you in the shoulder and then you can tell me how you think it feels." He glared at him.

"Fair enough."

"Will she be okay?" Nicolai looked down at his fiancée.

Ctephanyi put her hand on Angelina's head. "She will be fine, but she may have a few questions for us once she wakes up."

Nicolai nodded.

Ctephanyi motioned for him to give her his hand. She touched it tenderly and within a few moments it was completely healed. She laid her hand over Daniel's shoulder and he grinned. "Well that's a nice gift to have."

"Some days." She laughed.

"Will she remember me when she wakes up?" he questioned.

She sat quietly for a moment. "I hope not."

His eyes widened. "Why would you say that?"

She stood up and sighed. "Daniel, if she remembers you now, I'm not so sure you'll be able to stop her from destroying the world."

Everyone stared at Ctephanyi in silence. She was hiding something from them...something terrible. None of them wanted to ask her because none of them wanted to know the terrible truth of what awaited them in the days yet to come.

Chapter 24
Marked

I awoke with a jolt and jumped up. My heart pounded angrily against my chest and I looked around the empty campsite. Where had everyone gone?

"Nicolai?" I called out, "Jeremiah, where are you?"

"You're too late, I'm afraid," a familiar voice called out from behind me.

I spun around and took a step back. "Tristan."

He gave me a wicked smile and bowed before me. "My Queen."

"I'm not your anything," I growled.

He smirked. "You will be very soon."

"Not in this lifetime."

"See, that's where you're wrong." He laughed.

I watched him curiously. "What are you talking about?"

He walked out of the brush and sat down on the fallen log, "You see, my dear, your soul has already been reborn. If you were to die in this lifetime you couldn't come back."

"So," I muttered. "Who says I would even want to come back again?"

He glanced up at me, an evil twinkle in his emerald-green eyes. "You'll want to come back, trust me."

"Please, enlighten me as to why I would want to return," I taunted.

"It's quite simple really," he scoffed. "You'll want to save your unborn children."

I felt faint. "What did you just say?"

He stood up, dusted his pants off and came towards me. "Angelina, this world has a funny way of"—he paused for a moment— "bringing people together."

We stood staring at each other momentarily before he reached for my stomach.

"Don't touch me," I hissed, stumbling backwards.

"I want to show you something."

"What could you possibly want to show me?"

"You have a new little 'addition' to your body, correct?" he asked.

"How did you know that?" I replied, wrapping my arms around my stomach protectively.

"Because you've been marked," he answered.

"Marked?"

"You're meant for something greater, something so much more than I could have ever imagined."

I felt the little star shaped mark begin to tingle. I had almost forgotten about it until he had brought it up.

"Angelina, if you stand by my side, we can rule this world together."

I grimaced. "Why is it that all villains want to rule the world? I mean, can't you guys find something else to do? Like open up a casino or something?"

He chuckled, "May I?"

I watched him, and though I didn't want him to touch me, I let him.

He laid his hand across my stomach and his eyes widened. "Twins!"

My eyes widened right along with his. "What?"

He bent down and lifted my shirt up slightly. He wrapped his arms around my waist and put his ear on my bare belly. "Three heart beats—a boy, a girl, and yours."

I pulled away from him and shook my head. "Impossible."

"By now you should've learned that nothing is impossible."

Could it be true? Was I pregnant? No, I couldn't be. Could I?

"Stand by me, Angelina, I can protect you and the ones you carry."

I began to pace back and forth. It would explain a lot, my sudden emotional inconsistency with Nicolai, my angry outbursts with Daniel...

Tristan came up behind me and put his hand on my shoulder. "Angelina..."

I paused, a tear rolling lazily down my cheek. "What?" I asked, my voice cracking.

I felt his warm breath against the side of my face. "Let me take the worries from your heart. Let me silence your thoughts and take away your pain."

I closed my eyes, "I can't," I whispered.

He kissed my neck softly. "Let me love you like no man has ever loved you." He turned me around slowly. "I can offer you something nobody else can."

"What could you possibly offer me, Tristan?"

"I can offer you the world," he promised. "I can give you everything you've ever wanted."

I moaned softly as I felt his lips lightly touch mine. They were hard and stern. "Tristan, I…"

He caressed my face with his warm hand. "Let me give you the world. Let me take away your pain."

I felt his lips against mine again, this time more forceful. His kiss was so hungry and unforgiving. Nicolai's ember eyes flashed in my mind and I pushed Tristan away. "Get away from me," I screamed. "No, I will never be yours!"

His emerald eyes hardened. "You're a stupid girl. If you die, who is going to take care of your children? I can give you the gift of everlasting life."

My hand rose in the air and a surge of electric energy escaped from it, hitting Tristan square in the chest. He flew backwards, crashing into a tree behind him. It splintered and shook its branches in shock. "I may not live forever, but I'll live long enough to raise my children in a world that I will fight to protect and keep safe for them," I hissed.

"You'll fail," he promised, pulling himself up.

I stood my ground and held my head up proudly. "No, I won't Tristan, it's you who will fail."

"You've forgotten one little thing, my dear," he said. He wiped the blood splatter from his mouth. "Being half human will be your downfall. Your emotions will get the best of you."

"We'll see about that," I threatened.

"Yes, we sure will," he answered back before disappearing into the misty morning air of the dense forest, the crimson moss hiding his footsteps behind him.

I stood proudly for a moment, making sure he was no longer in the area before falling to my knees. I put my head in my hands and sobbed quietly. Not only did I have a world to save, but I had to protect the life of my unborn children. How would I tell Nicolai? What would he say? Would it scare him away? Was I ready to be a mother?

The questions swarming throughout my mind began to make my head hurt. I took a deep breath and wiped the tears from my face. I stood back up and sighed. When the time was right I would tell him, that's all I could do.

"Angelina, believe in yourself," a faint voice ordered. "It's time to wake up and do what you came back here to do."

I looked at the blue sky above me. "What did I come back here to do?"

"You came back to save humanity. You came back to bring love and peace to the world around you." The breeze carried the voice through the treetops, "What you carry is the key and they're meant to bring an end to all that is wrong."

"But I don't know if I'm ready," I called out to the whisper within the trees.

"There's only one way to find out," it whispered. "Wake up and do the right thing."

"The right thing?" I questioned.

"Wake up, Angelina." The voice grew faint. "Wake up and show the world that you're here to protect them. Show them all…"

Chapter 25
Old Friends

I opened my eyes and jumped up with a jolt. This time, instead of seeing an empty campsite I found curious eyes staring back at me. I sighed and calmed my heart.

Nicolai was at my side in a flash. "Angelina, are you okay?" he asked, worry heavy in his voice.

I stared at him and wrapped my arms around my stomach protectively. How was I going to tell him? I nodded and turned around. I just couldn't face him.

"Angelina?" I heard Bethani's sweet voice beckon. "Can I show you something I found earlier in the woods?"

I was relieved to follow her into the woods. I just couldn't deal with the secret I was keeping from the one I loved and the father of my children. Children? Did I really just think that? Oh crap, what if he read my thoughts? Wait, he promised he wouldn't do that anymore.

"Angelina," Bethani chimed in, breaking up my thoughts. "This way."

I gave her a slight smile and continued following her until we came upon an enormous moss-covered tree. She walked towards it and motioned for me to follow her. She disappeared behind it and I heard a soft giggle. I felt my eyebrows rise slightly and peeked my head around the tree curiously.

"He's been waiting for you." She giggled again.

A lump formed in my throat and I flung my arms around a familiar face. "Mathias!"

He hugged me tightly and kissed my cheek. "Angelina, you're..." He stood back and stared at me in surprise. His eyes ran through a multitude of colors. "...carrying twins!"

"Um, I..."

They both stared at me in surprise.

"I...well...yes, I am." I nodded.

"Angelina!" Bethani shrieked, her long blonde curls bouncing up and down with her in excitement.

"Shh!" I held a finger to my lips. "I don't want anyone else to know just yet."

"I'm so happy for you!" She hugged me tightly.

"Bethani." I struggled. "I can't breathe."

She laughed and let me go. "I'm going to plan for you what the humans call a baby shower!"

I laughed. "Okay."

"I've seen all kinds of pictures on the internet regarding things such as that." She giggled. "I'm so excited! Babies!"

I shook my head. "You have to promise me you won't say anything to Nicolai."

The smile disappeared from her face. "Why, are they not his? Are they Jeremiah's?"

"Bethani!" I laughed again. "Of course they're Nicolai's!"

"Whew, okay...I just don't know why you wouldn't want to tell him," she said, eyeing me curiously.

"She's afraid he'll leave her," Mathias interrupted.

She shook her head, her lavender eyes twinkling with excitement. "Oh, Angelina, Nicolai would never leave you."

"Fear does funny things to men. Wouldn't you agree, Mathias?" I asked.

"You're right," he agreed. "I shouldn't have left your side."

"I understood why you had to leave." I smiled. "Humanity wasn't really your thing."

He lowered his eyes and repeated, "I shouldn't have left your side."

"So, what are you going to name them?" Bethani chimed in.

I glanced at her and laughed. "I don't know yet."

Bethani put a finger to her chin in wonder. "I wonder if they're boys or girls."

Mathias, feeding into her happy bubble, said, "It's one of each."

"One of each?!" she shrieked again, "just like you and Daniel!" She instantly covered her mouth and looked down. "I'm sorry...I didn't mean to say that."

I stared at her in horror. "What did you just say?"

She kicked at the leaves and looked away.

"Bethani?"

She sighed. "I promised I wouldn't tell you, but this excitement...I just can't seem to contain myself."

"Angelina."

"Yes, Mathias?" I asked, not taking my eyes off Bethani.

"Take my hand," he offered, "I want to show you something."

Bethani kept her head down and continued kicking at the leaves and moss that covered the ground. I turned to look at him and grabbed his hand. I let out a gasp as images of Daniel and I filled my mind. Memories of us as children came flooding back. I felt a tear slide down my cheek. It was true, he was my twin brother. Mathias' eyes were ice white. "Why didn't he ever come for me?" I questioned, another tear falling down my cheek.

He held out his other hand and, without hesitation, I grabbed it. A memory of Daniel trying to talk me out of my planned death plagued my mind. He had tried so hard to get me to change my mind. The pain in his eyes as he followed through with my wishes left me feeling sick. "I asked him to do it," I whispered.

Mathias let go of my hands. "Yes, you did."

"Why did he listen to me?" I shook my head, unable to free myself from the painful look I had seen on Daniel's face. "Why didn't he just say no?"

"Because he loved you." Mathias smiled. "In fact, he still loves you and that, my dear, is why he continues to beat himself up for what he's done."

"But it wasn't his fault," I said, guilt spreading through me like a wildfire. "I asked him to do it."

"I know." He nodded. "He listened to you and your blood fell on his hands."

I breathed in deeply and exhaled slowly. "And all this time I thought he hated me."

Bethani let out a giggle. "Can I tell him he's going to be an uncle?"

We both looked at her and yelled out, "No!"

She looked at us wide-eyed and smiled. "Okay, but can we teach them to call me Aunt Bethani?"

I rolled my eyes and nodded. "Sure."

She jumped up and down in excitement. "I can't wait!"

"We should be getting back." I laughed. "They'll be excited to see you, Mathias."

He frowned. "I'm afraid I can't go back with you."

"What?" I looked at him confused. "Why not?"

"I came to warn you."

"Warn me about what?" I asked, watching the colors of his eyes change to light gray.

"She's working with him."

"Who?"

He turned his head, fear crawling into his gray eyes. "I must find Stephen."

"Wait, who's working with him?"

He turned his head and frowned. "I must go."

"No, Mathias, wait." I reached out towards him. He ignored my plea and disappeared into the forest.

"Angelina?" a gruff voice called out behind me.

I turned around and stared at the man before me. I admired his features. The way his dark hair fell over his face; it was wild like mine. The same curve of his lips, the way his nose flared slightly when he talked…there was no mistaking it. He was my brother.

"I should go," Bethani said with a smirk. "I'll be back at the camp…planning."

I glanced over at her and rolled my eyes. "Remember, you promised."

She flashed a big smile, "I know, I won't say a word. I swear."

She ran off through the brush, leaving Daniel and I alone in silence.

"Can we talk?" he asked, shoving his hands into his jeans pockets.

I nodded my head and slid down the soft, moss-covered tree. I patted the leaves next to me. He walked over and slid down next to me. For a moment, we both stared off into the forest in silence. The air around us was warm, with a cool breeze caressing our skin every so often.

Daniel finally broke the silence. "I need to tell you something."

I nodded, afraid to look at him, "Okay."

"I need you to know that I'm your…"

Suddenly an arrow came whizzing through the forest and struck him in the chest. He let out a loud groan as another one embedded itself in his stomach.

"No!" I screamed pushing him out of the way of the third arrow that grazed the side of my shoulder.

Blood spewed out of his mouth as I used my strength to pull him to the other side of the tree. I cautiously peeked my head around the tree and saw the hooded archer flee into the forest.

"Angelina," Daniel whispered.

I went back to his side and pulled at the arrow stuck in his chest, "Daniel, it's okay, just stay awake."

"Angelina, I'm so sorry," he continued, "I shouldn't have listened to you."

"We can talk about this later."

"No." he put his hand over mine, "I shouldn't have let you die."

"It's in the past, Daniel, just don't move," I urged.

"Let me go."

I looked at him in surprise. "No."

"Angelina, let me go."

I felt a tear slide down my face. "No, I need you."

He smiled and wiped the tear from my face. "I love you, sis. You're all I've ever had."

With that he closed his eyes. I shook him slightly, "Daniel?!" I shook him again. "Daniel, you can't leave me!" I took a deep breath. "No, I won't do as you ask. I won't let you go." I stood up and let the electricity flow through my body. I thought of Daniel carrying me on his back through the forest, I thought of him protecting me, keeping me safe from all the horrors of the world. It was my turn to do him a favor. It was my turn to do the protecting and show my twin brother just how much he really meant to me.

Chapter 26
Broken Promises

"Angelina's been gone awhile," Nicolai noted, pacing back and forth impatiently.

"I'm sure she and Bethani are just having some girl time," Ctephanyi said without looking up at him. Snow let out a soft whimper and lay her head across Ctephanyi's lap.

He ignored his mother's words. "Maybe I should go see what's keeping them."

Just then he saw Bethani's blonde curls bopping up and down in the distance. His heart sank once he realized that she had come back alone. "Where's Angelina?" he asked, as she made her way towards them.

She gave him a sly smile. "She's talking with Daniel."

He let out a sigh of relief and sat down. He glanced back up at Bethani. "Is she okay?"

"She's better than you think," Bethani said.

He shook his head—she was so weird sometimes. His mind wandered back to the woman he loved. Things had been somewhat indifferent between he and Angelina. He could sense the tension between them and though he so desperately wanted to poke around in her thoughts, he had promised her he wouldn't.

Snow lifted her head abruptly. Her ears flattened back and her white fur began to slowly stand up on end. She let out a growl and jumped to her feet. Her tail stiffened and her growl deepened as she stared into the forest at something unseen. Suddenly, she let out a long howl and ran into the forest.

"What's wrong with her?" Jeremiah questioned, his gaze shifting towards Snow.

Nicolai stood up, followed by his father and Josiah. Ctephanyi's eyes began to brighten as she searched the forest for signs of life. "Something's wrong with Angelina," she commented. "Snow was bred specifically for Angelina. She can feel everything Angelina feels."

Jeremiah hurried to his feet, "Where is she?"

"Nicolai." Ctephanyi motioned to him.

He looked at his mother, "What do you need me to do?"

"I need you to read her thoughts."

His eyes widened in surprise. "No, I can't. I promised."

"Nicolai, it's imperative you do this," she urged. "The forest is too large for us to just go looking for her."

"Why can't *you* just read her thoughts?" Jeremiah questioned Ctephanyi, his adrenaline beginning to surge throughout his muscular body. He felt his muscles begin to twitch in anticipation.

She gave him an icy glare that sent shivers down his spine, "She is the daughter of Hecate."

"So?" he replied, not understanding.

"Her mind is shielded now that she knows who she is," she said. "The only person who can read her thoughts is Nicolai."

He glanced at Nicolai in jealous disgust. "Why him?"

"Because she loves him," she answered, annoyed by his numerous questions. "She lets her guard down with him, therefore he's the only person that can get through."

He shrugged. "Whatever."

"Mother, I can't. I promised," Nicolai repeated.

"Nicolai, she's in danger." Elias interjected, "What is more important—hurt feelings or her life?"

He felt the fire surge throughout his ember eyes. The thought of Angelina being in danger sickened him. Even though he had promised her that he would never again pry into her mind, he knew his father was right. "Okay," he agreed and began to listen to the forest that surrounded them.

"What do you hear?" her father asked, worry heavyset on his face.

"Silence," he instructed, motioning for everyone in the camp to be quiet. It was harder to read her thoughts when she wasn't around him.

He knelt and placed the palm of his hand on the soft ground. The vibrations of life within the forest began to fill his mind. He concentrated on finding his target and let his senses take control. He could hear the light breeze comb its long fingers through the tall tree tops. He felt the small vibration of chipmunks scurrying through the brush and the steady beat of whitetail deer. He sensed a human female full of excitement and fear. He concentrated on her and felt her fast and unsteady footsteps glide through the forest. He envisioned her in a hooded, black cloak with a bow.

"Be on your guard, someone is nearby," he ordered, continuing to watch the hooded figure in his mind flee through the forest.

"Who is it, Nicolai?" Ctephanyi asked, peering into the forest.

"I'm not sure." He raised his other hand. "Wait."

He caught a very low vibration nearby. He turned his full attention towards it—his eyes widening as he realized it was the faint sound of a heartbeat and not one, but three of them! Two seemed to be low and steady while the third one seemed to be angry and out of control. He smiled, he knew that noise well—it was Angelina's heartbeat. The other two, however, were small and faint, almost childlike. They reminded him of the heartbeats he had heard during his stint as a doctor in the maternity ward when he was searching for the perfect vessel for Angelina's soul.

A sudden realization washed over him, and his stature weakened.

Jeremiah let out an impatient sigh. "Did you find her?"

Nicolai felt his hand tremble and tried to maintain his composure. "Yes, I found *them*."

"Well," Jeremiah stared at him dumbfounded. "Where are they?"

Nicolai swallowed the lump that had formed in his throat and stood up, nonchalantly running his hands through his messy black hair. He turned his back towards them as a tear fell down his rugged cheek. He reached his hand up and caught it unknowingly. His mind was in shock as the overwhelming amount of emotions took ahold of him and coursed throughout his body.

Ctephanyi, moved by her son's show of emotion, went to his aid. "What's wrong, my dear boy?" she questioned, putting a delicate hand on his shoulder.

Bethani stared at them in silence. She knew what he had heard and was somewhat disappointed she hadn't been the one to tell him.

Josiah cleared his throat impatiently. "Nicolai, where are my children?"

Nicolai felt an invisible force lift his arm and point towards the direction he'd heard the heartbeats come from. Without hesitation, Josiah took off at full speed, followed by Jeremiah and a snarling Snow.

Bethani watched them disappear into the forest and took a step to follow them. She turned back momentarily and studied Nicolai curiously. She could sense the confusion, excitement, anger, and apprehension emitting from his usual cool demeanor. His handsome face had hardened as he tried to come to terms with the revelation he had just witnessed.

He turned and looked at her. "You knew," he stated in a monotone voice.

She nodded. "Yes, but I made a promise."

"So did I." He shrugged his mother's hand off his shoulder. "But I broke mine."

Bethani watched him disappear into the forest behind the others and observed a look of confusion enter into Ctephanyi's eyes. "You read his mind."

She took a step back and Elias wrapped his arms around his wife protectively. "We must keep her safe," Ctephanyi whispered to Elias in shock. "She's carrying something so very precious. Our bloodline."

Elias nodded in agreement. "We will."

Bethani sighed at the love that crept into their eyes. She smiled to herself and thought about how so much had changed since their first meeting with Nicolai's parents. She wrapped her slender arms around herself and hoped the path of change they traveled down continued in a positive manner.

Ctephanyi shook off her moment of human weakness and stood proudly next to her husband. "Shall we join them?"

Bethani nodded and headed into the forest followed by the two people who had started out as the ultimate enemies. With the winds of change swirling through the air, a new enemy had emerged, and she knew it was only a matter of time before they would encounter him and discover what the definition of *enemy* truly was.

Chapter 27
Ambushed

The electricity surged through my body as I commanded the moss to wrap around the arrows that were stuck in Daniel's stomach and chest. Anger spun its wicked web inside my mind as the arrows disappeared inside the thick moss and blood oozed from the gaping holes that were left behind. I would make whoever had done this pay, but right now, time was against me and I knew I had to work quickly or Daniel would die.

I leaned over him and kissed his forehead, "Today will not be the day death greets you with open arms, because I will not allow it to happen."

Gagging, I laid my hands over the blood-soaked wound. I took a deep breath and looked away—these pregnancy changes were proving to be quite annoying. Shaking off the queasiness, I tried to concentrate. The power I had grown used to ran through my fingertips and seeped into his chest. The wound began to heal itself and I let out a sigh of relief. A few moments later, both wounds had been healed, leaving bright red scars in their places.

"Daniel?" I whispered in his ear. "Can you hear me?"

He stirred slightly.

"Daniel," I whispered again. "Wake up."

His eyes popped open and he jumped up and swung at the air.

I laughed. "Woah, killer, calm down."

He had a bewildered look on his face as he searched the forest for the perpetrator who had attacked them.

"They're gone."

He looked down at me, "You're sure?"

Taking one more look around, I nodded. "Yes, I don't sense his presence any longer."

"Are you hurt?" he asked, scanning my body for any open wounds.

"I'm fine," I promised.

He looked me over once again and laid his head back against the soft moss that ran up the tree behind him, "If anything happened to you again…"

I laid my hand over his. "Nothing is going to happen to me."

He shook his head in defeat and I could tell he was trying to hide his emotions.

I nudged him. "Can I tell you a secret?"

He leaned forward and smiled. "A secret?"

"Mmmhmm," I smiled deviously.

"What kind of secret?"

"The good kind," I answered with a smirk.

His eyes lit up. "Sure!"

"I know that you're my twin brother."

His eyes filled with tears and for a moment we bathed in the silence between us. It was an endearing moment, and I would forever hold in my heart.

"You know?"

"I do." I nodded. "Want to hear another secret?"

"Another one?" he stared at me in surprise.

"Yup," I laughed.

"Well…uhm…" he fidgeted uncomfortably. "Sure?"

An old memory filtered into my mind. Daniel had been blessed with the gift of sight and could see things unseen to others. Excited, I grabbed his hand and lay it across my stomach. "What do you see?"

"Angelina, I can't," he said.

"I give you permission to use your gift on me."

"I'm not sure that I should."

"Why not?" I nudged him again, "It won't hurt."

He sighed and closed his eyes. A moment later a tear fell down his face and he smiled. "I'm going to be an uncle."

I nodded and felt my own eyes begin to well up with tears. He grabbed my hand and for a moment we stared into each other's eyes, passing old memories and thoughts between the two of us.

"Angelina!" A frantic voice called out from behind us, "Angelina, where are you?!"

I snapped back to reality and poked my head around the corner of the tree. I felt a wet tongue on my face as Snow pounced on top of me. I laughed and nuzzled my face next to hers. Soft fur tickled my cheeks as she continued to shower me with puppy kisses. I knew I hadn't been gone long, but I would've sworn she had gained at least fifteen pounds since I had last seen her.

"Angelina?" I heard my father ask breathlessly in between a barrage of wet, sloppy dog kisses.

"Yes?" I laughed, pushing Snow towards Daniel. Her tail stiffened as she proceeded with caution towards him.

"Come on, girl." He patted his leg.

She wagged her tail, still somewhat unsure and sniffed his leg. A moment later Daniel found himself covered in Snow's wet kisses.

"She knows." He laughed.

"She's a smart dog," I commented, watching the two of them enjoy each other's company.

"Angelina!" Jeremiah called out from the distance.

"Are you okay?" my father asked, bending down next to me.

"I'm okay," I answered, looking over at Daniel.

My father followed my gaze, "Daniel, you were hurt!"

"Huh?" he looked up, surprised, "What are you talking about?"

"The scars!" our father pointed towards Daniel's chest.

Daniel looked down and examined the new scars that graced his muscular body. "Well look at that," he said gruffly, not surprised.

"You didn't know?"

He looked at our father and smiled. "No, I suppose I didn't." He shrugged.

I knew better than to think he could care less. In fact, I knew that Daniel and I would be having a conversation about this later on and I was okay with that.

"Angelina, what happened?" Jeremiah asked breathlessly, his muscles twitching in excitement.

"I'm not quite sure," I answered honestly.

"You're not sure?"

"Well, as we were talking someone decided to take a moment and shoot some arrows our way," I replied nonchalantly.

Jeremiah's bright blue eyes grew dark with anger. "Someone tried to kill you?"

"Well, yes…I suppose they did."

He stared at me and I could tell by the look on his face he was trying to restrain himself from unleashing a slew of obscenities. "Angelina, you don't find this somewhat troubling? I mean, look at Daniel's chest!" he pointed out. He reached down and grabbed my hand, "Look at your hands, they're covered in blood!"

I looked down and frowned at the dried blood that covered my pale hands. "Jeremiah, we're alive." I looked over at Daniel and smiled. "That's all that matters."

Jeremiah let out a frustrated sigh and cursed under his breath.

"Jeremiah, calm down," my father urged. "There's nothing we can do now."

"Sure, there is," he hissed. "We can find whoever did this and tear them into pieces."

"But Jeremiah," Bethani's sweet voice chimed in from behind him. "That would make a mess. Don't you think an arrow to the head would be much cleaner?"

"Or perhaps just tearing off the legs would suffice," Ctephanyi smirked, overhearing the conversation.

"We could always sic Snow on them," Elias offered. "I hear she's quite deadly."

Snow barked loudly, and they all let out a hearty laugh, even Jeremiah, who had found humor in their comments.

I looked at the smiling faces that surrounded me and noticed one face was missing—Nicolai. I peered past them and saw nothing. My heart sank, but I knew he would be back. We were destined to be together and nothing could separate us, not even death.

I glanced back up at the people I cared so deeply for. They had so much love in their hearts and I knew that any one of them would do anything to protect me. I just prayed I could return the favor when the time came for me to make my choice.

Chapter 28
Evil Imitations

The sun set and another day had passed us by. We were running out of time and so much had happened in the past few days. I sat down to reflect on it and smiled to myself, knowing everything would turn out the way it was supposed to. I was confident in the love that I felt for Nicolai, who had gone missing the night before. I was confident he was off looking for whoever had tried to kill us. I was confident in the love I felt for the twins that grew in my womb, and I was confident in the love that I felt for Daniel.

I started my morning off feeling rather queasy and passed on the breakfast that Jeremiah had so kindly cooked up for us. I was tired and moody, so I tried to rest up as best I could underneath a large tree that provided shade from the sun's warm rays. The ground was lumpy and uncomfortable, so no matter which way I laid, I just couldn't manage to fall asleep.

"Come," I whispered, coaxing the moss to comfort my aching back. It snaked across the ground and cradled my tired body under its soft tendrils. I breathed a sigh of relief as the sandman finally graced me with sound sleep.

For the first time in days I slept without dreaming. No nightmares, no glimpses of the future. It was wonderful.

I felt soft hands shake my shoulders gently. "Angelina?"

"Hmm?" I groaned, not wanting to open my eyes.

"You need to get up, we have to get moving," a familiar voice urged.

I groaned again. "Five more minutes?"

"Five more minutes and I'm going to let Snow bathe you in kisses," the voice warned.

I knew that voice well—it was the man I loved, the father of my unborn children—it was Nicolai. My eyes flew open and I found myself staring into his gorgeous fiery orange eyes. "You're back," I breathed slowly.

He kissed me softly. "I love you."

"I love you too." I kissed him in return. "And I'm sorry."

He caressed my cheek lovingly. "My world would be no more if you were not in it."

Guilt began to swarm my thoughts. "Nicolai, there's something..."

"We have to go," Jeremiah called out frantically. "We have to go now!"

I pushed past Nicolai and jumped to my feet. "What's wrong?"

"What isn't wrong?" Jeremiah pointed towards the sky.

He was right, the blue sky had begun to darken in the distance, but it wasn't due to storm clouds—it was something else and it was moving at a tremendous speed.

I stared at the fast-approaching darkness. "What is that?"

Nicolai grabbed my hand and pulled me lightly, "Jeremiah's right, we have to go."

Snow yelped ahead of us. "Snow!" I whistled, beckoning her to come to me. She let out another yelp followed by a deep growl. I let go of Nicolai's hand and ran towards the sound. "Snow, come on, girl," I called out. "Where are you?"

In one swift motion, Bethani had her bow in hand, ready to fire. "Angelina, watch out!" she said, an arrow flying past my face.

I ducked immediately, and by the horrified look on her face, I knew it was something very bad.

Snow yelped again, and I refocused on finding her. Stumbling over a fallen log, I flew forward, my hands grazing across something sharp. Then I saw her. Off in the distance, I could make out a small ball of white fluff. Ignoring the gashes on my palms, I pulled myself up off the ground.

"Get down!" Bethani rammed into me, and we both slid across the hard ground. An arrow whizzed past the both of us. Whatever or whoever this was obviously had it out for me.

"Cover me."

Bethani nodded. "Ready?" she whispered.

I nodded.

"Now!" she screamed, aiming her bow at something nearby. She let her arrow fly, and I ran as fast as my short legs would carry me. Bethani's scream had caught Snow's attention and she began running towards us.

She let out a long, vicious howl, her tail wagging triumphantly behind her. I peered past my white fluffy friend and saw what appeared to be a human figure lying in the fetal position on the ground. Snow turned back momentarily to check and make sure her attacker stayed in place and in one swift movement, disappeared into the brush behind me.

Moving forward cautiously, I felt my face twist into sheer surprise. "Stephen?"

His eyes flew open and he hopped to his feet. "Aw crap, I recognize that voice."

I stumbled backwards. "You're not hurt?" I asked, eying him up.

He snickered and dusted himself off. "Of course not."

"Then why were you curled into a ball on the ground?"

He rolled his eyes. "Because that blasted white ball of fluff wouldn't get off my nuts unless I let it win."

I couldn't help but let out a girlish giggle. "I thought you were invincible."

"Same annoying sense of humor, I see," he said.

Shooting him a snide look, I replied, "Yeah, I see your cocky demeanor hasn't changed much either."

He grew quiet.

"What's wrong?" I asked.

He glanced past me. Something had caught his eye. "Don't get mad at me, okay?"

"For what?"

"For this," he said, throwing his weight into me.

We both fell to the ground with a thud. With a disgusted look on my face, I pushed him off me, and looked around. Suddenly, something jumped through the brush and disappeared. "What was that?"

Stephen jumped to his feet. "You don't want to know."

"Of course I want to know."

He shrugged. "Fine, but you're not going to like it."

I stood up and shot him a cocky look. "There are quite a few things in this world that I don't like."

"Angelina."

"Stephen."

"Do we really have time for this?" I said.

He smirked. "I'm a vampire, I have all the time in the world."

"I can't believe you."

"Okay, that thing you just saw hop into that bush and disappear was a vapor demon."

"Okay, enlighten me. What is a vapor demon?" I asked.

For a split second, I thought he paled a little. And was that terror in his eyes?

He crouched down and picked up a handful of dried leaves. He stared at them before giving me an icy glare. "Every creature that has walked this Earth has evil in them whether they know it or not." He began to crush the dried leaves and opened his hand. The wind carried the small dried pieces through the air and they began to swirl around us. "A vapor demon sucks that evil out of you to temporarily use it against you to hurt the ones you love."

I stood in awe as the air grew stagnant and the tiny pieces fell to the ground. "So, these things are an imitation of us?"

He stood back up. "Somewhat."

"Where do they come from?"

"They can only be summoned by someone of great power."

"Tristan," I whispered.

"Ah, I see you've made another enemy. Surprise."

I rolled my eyes. "I'm about to make you my enemy," I snapped.

He let out a hearty laugh. "Oh, Angelina, you do make me smile."

I shifted my weight uncomfortably. "How do we get rid of these vapor things?"

"You have to overcome the evil with the goodness you carry within you."

"So basically, you stand no chance." I smirked.

"Ha…funny."

"Angelina!" I heard Nicolai's voice boom through the forest.

Stephen smiled his arrogant smile. "Oh, it looks like Hercules is coming to save the day."

I didn't even entertain his snide comment. "I'm over here," I called out.

Nicolai was next to me in a flash. "Are you okay?" he asked, a worried look on his handsome face.

I smiled up at him reassuringly. "I'm fine."

"Stephen." He nodded in respect.

"Hercules." Stephen nodded back.

"What?"

I laughed. "He thinks he's being funny."

"I see," he stated, emotionless. "Where's everyone else?"

I looked around, "I'm not sure."

"You're positive you're okay?" he asked again.

"Yes, I'm certain."

"Always overprotective, aren't ya?" Stephen quipped.

Nicolai pulled me in close to him. "I don't know what I would do if I lost you again."

I kissed him sweetly. "You won't."

Stephen made a gagging noise behind us. "Get a room."

"If only we could." I shot him an evil smile.

"See, everyone has evil in them, Angelina." His arrogance faded. "Even you."

Chapter 29
Caught

Jeremiah looked around. "Where's Angelina?" he called out.

Bethani pulled another arrow back and let it fly, "I don't know."

He scanned the forest and yelled, "Angelina!"

"She's not here," Bethani noted, reaching for another arrow from her quiver.

Jeremiah felt a sharp pain in his shoulder and turned around. His eyes widened at the sight in front of him. "What the hell are these things?" he asked in awe.

"They're vapor demons," Bethani said, not missing a beat.

"It looks just like you!" he commented, pulling the arrow out of his shoulder blade.

"It is me, only a much more unpleasant version."

"Is that even possible?" he asked, ducking as another arrow flew past him.

"What do you think?" she asked, nodding toward the bloody wound on his shoulder.

"Well, how do you kill these things?"

"Aim for their hearts, but be careful not to hit with hatred, as that's what they feed off."

"How am I not supposed to hit this thing with hatred? It's trying to kill me."

"Let the goodness in your heart shine through."

"You're sure this will work?" he questioned.

She shot another arrow into the vapor demon, this time striking its heart, and it imploded.

"I guess so." He pulled out his hunting knife and ran through the forest. Hearing a low growl, he assumed Snow was nearby along with another vapor demon. He moved cautiously through the brush, his knife by his side. He wasn't about to let one of these weird vapor things get another cheap shot.

"Jeremiah, watch out!" Angelina's father warned from behind a large oak.

It was too late; he felt weightless. His arms unconsciously stretched up over his head and his knife fell to the ground. He tried to speak, but no sound came out. His feet dangled as he struggled to regain control of his body. Josiah's eyes were full of horror as he watched silently from the ground below.

In an instant, Josiah was dangling in the air next to Jeremiah. His arms, stretched up over his head. Evil laughter filled the air. "Two of the most important men in Angelina's life are two of the weakest."

"Put them down," Daniel's voice boomed from the ground below.

Tristan turned around to face him, a sly smirk on his face, "My, oh my, don't you look familiar."

"Let them go," Daniel warned.

Tristan stared at him in amusement. "Don't be a hero."

"Don't be a dick," Daniel retorted.

Tristan let out a hearty laugh, "Wow, using grown up words, now are we? Finally fit into our big boy pants, I see."

Daniel's muscles twitched in anticipation. "I'm not going to ask you again."

Tristan strutted towards him cockily. "Tell me, what are you going to do? Do you really want to join them?" He pointed to the air. "And leave your sister all alone again? Is that what you want? Because I can most certainly make that happen."

Fear flickered through Daniel's eyes at the thought of abandoning Angelina and for a moment, he let his guard down.

"Don't like that option too much, I see."

Daniel looked at the ground and then looked up at Jeremiah. "I'm sorry," he whispered.

"What a bunch of cowards." Tristan laughed, "The three of you are indeed quite pitiful."

Daniel stared back down at the ground without saying a word while Jeremiah continued to try and regain control over his body.

"How did you all think you were going to protect her when you can't even protect yourselves?"

"I can answer that question," a female voice said behind him.

He turned around and smiled. "How nice to see you, Ctephanyi."

She nodded. "Now why don't you put the boys down?"

His eyes darted past her as Elias made his way towards them. "Ah, I see you've brought your bodyguard."

She smirked. "Bodyguard? My dear boy, this would be my husband, Elias."

His eyes widened. "So, he lives."

Elias nodded, "That seems to be the case."

"Well…" Tristan sighed, "I do appear to be outnumbered, don't I?"

Elias put his arm around Ctephanyi protectively. "You could say that."

Tristan put a finger to his lips thoughtfully. "I could put them down and save myself the trouble of having to fight with you or…"

"Or what?" Ctephanyi asked, her white eyes beginning to glow.

"Or I could do this," he snapped his fingers. In an instant he was gone, along with Josiah and Jeremiah.

"No!" she screamed in anger. "How dare he!"

"We'll get them back," Elias reassured.

Daniel nodded in agreement. "We'll make him pay."

She looked at them both, her bright eyes dimming. "What are we going to tell Angelina?"

Elias wrapped his arms around his wife and held her close. "The truth."

Chapter 30
The Truth

Something was wrong; I could feel it in the pit of my stomach. Nicolai glanced over at me, a look of knowing on his handsome face. My eyes darted over to Stephen who seemed to also sense something was amiss.

"We need to go," I muttered. "Something's not right."

Suddenly Bethani came running towards us. "Angelina, Tristan's taken your father and Jeremiah."

"No," I whispered, my cheeks beginning to grow warm with frustration.

"Where did he take them?" Nicolai asked, his voice filling with anger.

"They disappeared into thin air," Ctephanyi's voice called out from behind us.

"It was like they were there one minute and gone the next," Daniel's gruff voice chimed in.

I turned towards Ctephanyi. "Where would he take them?"

She frowned, her light eyes dulling. "There's only one place he could've taken them."

I stared at her in surprise.

She smiled. "You're wondering how I know that."

I nodded.

"A very long time ago someone once told me that past performance is indicative of future behavior."

My mouth dropped open and I realized that "someone" was most likely my mother as that had been a phrase embedded into my memory.

She turned her attention towards Nicolai. "We need to go back to the beginning, to the place where it all started—the cave."

He nodded, an understanding in his beautiful sunset-colored eyes. "Of course, that's where he would take them."

I looked at them in suspicion. "And where would this place be?"

She turned her attention back towards me, "Angelina, do you remember the cave where I came to you when you were a young child?"

"Yes, how could I forget?" I replied. I had the faint memory of her calming touch on my cool cheek the night I had become lost in the woods in search of my father.

"That is the place it all began."

I looked over at Daniel who shrugged in confusion. "The cave?"

Ctephanyi took a step towards me and whispered in my ear, "*Remember, Angelina, remember.*"

Her melodic words were like a fine-tuned song that began to play repeatedly in my head. I grew dizzy as the world seemed to slip away while an older, more distant past came rushing back. I closed my eyes and let the cool, crisp air rush against my flushed cheeks. I let the dampness of the dark cave surround me. I remembered this place. The despair I had felt as a child filled my soul once again and my eyes flew open.

"Impossible," I whispered, my breath misting in the cool air. I looked around and realized I was alone. The cave was dark and just as unforgiving as I had remembered it, only this time there was no sweet voice—no bright eyes watching me from within the darkness.

I stumbled forward, my hands gliding across the rough, rocky wall to steady myself. My heart beat in my ears as the silence thickened around me. I continued, careful not to stumble over the broken boulders that littered the slick, muddy floor. Though I was older, I felt small and vulnerable in the large cave. How I wished for my strong, loving Nicolai to be by my side. I wished for the safety of my father and Jeremiah. Heck, I just wished for the normality of my old life, but it was too late for that now, wasn't it?

I refocused on the task at hand and continued blindly into the darkness. I tripped and stumbled forward, scraping my knees across the muddy ground. I sat down and cradled my head in my hands. "I can't do this," I whispered, tears of anger filling my eyes.

"*Angelina,*" a soft voice whispered from within the darkness.

I wiped my tears of anger away and listened. Deafening silence fell upon my ears. Just when I started to question my sanity, I heard it.

"*Angelina, be strong,*" it whispered lovingly.

I recognized that voice. It couldn't be…could it? I stood up and stared into the darkness. "Momma?" I whispered back. I listened and heard a slight humming noise. My heart stopped once I realized it was the tune I had heard a million times as a child. It was the one song that held so many special memories for me and my parents. It was the song that my father had used to win over my mother's heart: *Brown Eyed Girl.*

"Mom!" I called out, forcing my feet to stumble blindly down the muddy floor. Suddenly a dim light appeared in the distance. I shielded my eyes from the unfamiliar light as it moved closer. It floated through the air like a whisper through the wind.

"*Angelina.*"

I stared at the glowing orb in awe. "Mom?"

It bobbed through the damp air and settled momentarily in front of me. "*Don't be afraid.*"

I reached out to touch the light glow in front of me. It flew into the air, causing me to take a step backwards. My heart fluttered in my chest as I retracted my hand back to my side protectively.

"*Don't be afraid,*" it whispered again.

I swallowed my fear and continued to follow the soft glow through the winding darkness. A few moments later, I found myself standing outside what looked like the entrance to another portion of the cave.

"*Go inside,*" the loving voice persuaded.

I hesitated. I didn't want to leave the soft glow of my mother's light. It was as if her spirit had been placed in a star that had fallen from the sky to show me the secrets that had been hidden from my mind. I found comfort in her soft voice and was reminded of how much I truly missed her.

"I can't go," I said, choking back tears. "I can't lose you again."

The orb bobbed through the air, "*Angelina, you must go.*"

I shook my head. "Please don't make me leave you."

It stopped moving and pulsated close to my face. A warm sensation filled my body and I knew her soul had touched mine. "*Fear not, my daughter, for I will always be with you,*" her soft voice promised. "*Forever.*"

I felt a tear slide down my cool cheek and nodded. "Forever."

It bobbed towards the opening once again and I sighed. "Well, here goes nothing." I stepped inside the opening and nothing could have prepared me for what my eyes saw next.

Chapter 31
Connected

Nicolai stared at his mother who seemed pleased with herself He had witnessed that smirk many times before.

"What's wrong?" Daniel whispered with a soft nudge.

Startled, Nicolai looked down and shook his head. "I don't know. Something's not right."

"What do you mean?" he questioned, raising a brow in suspicion.

"She smirks." He nodded towards his mother. "But for what reason?"

"Do you think Angelina is okay?"

For a moment, he contemplated his answer and finally muttered, "I need to go."

"I'll take that as a no."

Nicolai felt a small hand rest upon his shoulder, "Fear not, my dear friend, for Angelina is safe."

"How are you so sure?" he asked the lavender-eyed Bethani.

She smiled sweetly at him. "Though your mother once walked the path of death and destruction, she now walks the path of righteousness and remains true to the goodness in her heart."

"Then why does she smirk?"

Bethani glanced at Ctephanyi and squeezed Nicolai's shoulder softly, "She sees what Angelina's currently seeing."

"Wait." He stared at her in surprise. "What do you mean she sees what Angelina is seeing?"

She let out a girlish giggle. "Right now, their minds are connected so that Ctephanyi may watch over her in spirit. What Angelina sees is shared between the two of them."

He glanced back at his mother and watched her facial expressions change. Her smirk curved up into a full-blown smile while a tear fell lazily down her pale cheek. In some sense, he was jealous. He wondered what she was seeing and could only imagine all the emotions she was feeling at that very moment. Sighing, he hoped that one day his mind would link with Angelina's, so he could feel the raw emotion he knew she carried within her.

Daniel nudged Nicolai's shoulder, breaking his train of thought. "So, do you think we'll stop Tristan?"

Nicolai wanted to say yes, but something nagged at the back of his head. The memory of Tristan and his mother flashed back into his mind. He looked at Daniel and hesitated. "At first I did…yes."

"What do you mean at first?"

"Well, the situation has changed."

Daniel grew quiet and cocked his eyebrow. "How so?"

"He's grown much more powerful now, and well…he's gained…" He paused before muttering, "bargaining chips."

Daniel frowned. "Yeah, you're right. Angelina's not going to give up easily though."

Nicolai smirked. "Yeah, isn't that the truth."

"You know, when we were little kids, I always knew she was special."

Nicolai glanced over at him, amused. "How so?"

"Well, she always seemed to have this aura around her," he said thoughtfully. "Once we were in the woods and we happened to come across a small fawn that had been left abandoned. It was severely emaciated and I knew if I didn't put it out of its misery that it would continue to suffer."

Nicolai watched as emotion from the old memory began to make its presence known on Daniel's rugged face.

"Angelina begged me to not to touch it, and I explained to her that it was for the best." He smiled momentarily as the memory replayed itself in his mind, "You know what she said to me?"

"What?" Nicolai answered, intrigued.

"She looked up at me, confidence in her big, innocent eyes and simply said: I will fix him. If you touch him, I will break you."

"Wow," Nicolai laughed. "Big words from such a little girl."

"Yeah." Daniel shoved his hands into his pockets.

"So, what did you do?"

He shrugged. "I let her fix him."

Nicolai let out a laugh. "That was probably a smart decision."

He nodded. "She has so much life in her, but…" his eyes grew dark and he looked down.

"But what?" Nicolai raised a brow.

"She has a dark side, too." He kicked at the ground. "One you do not want to see."

Nicolai stared at him curiously. "How so?"

"Where there is life, there will always be death, and that is something we can never change."

"What?"

Ctephanyi's voice chimed in, "We have to go."

Nicolai's gaze shifted to his mother. "Is something wrong?"

"Yes," she replied calmly.

He swallowed hard and drew in his breath. "What is it?"

"I know who the traitor is and they have Angelina. We must get to her before it's too late," Ctephanyi said.

Daniel's muscles began to twitch with anticipation. "Well, what are we waiting for?"

"Why, you boys, of course." Bethani's sweet voice interrupted.

The feeling that had been nagging at the back of Nicolai's head returned and he knew he had been right. Something was wrong. *What if his mother was one of the traitors and her smirk was because she had known all along what Angelina was walking into?* He had no idea what he was about to get into, but he knew he would do whatever it took to save the one person he knew had been made just for him.

Chapter 32
Best Friends

I looked around and let out a gasp. Before me stood my best friend, Marie. She looked at me and smiled. The shadows in the room hidden deep within the cave played across her pretty face. She pulled me in for a hug and I pushed her away. Something just didn't feel right.

"What are you doing here?" I questioned, still somewhat surprised by her appearance.

"The bigger question is, why you are here?" she asked in return.

Puzzled by her question, I debated whether I really wanted to tell her what—or should I say who—had led me to her.

She ran her finger down my cheek and turned around. "I know who you followed."

"You do?" I asked.

"I do," she replied, not turning around.

"How did you…"

"You're not the only one around here who is *special,* you know," she interrupted.

"Wait," I began, "I never said I was special."

She finally turned back around and raised her hand in protest. "You didn't have to say anything. It's all about the way you carry yourself, Angelina."

I fought back the anger that was beginning to course through my veins. "I don't carry myself any differently than I had before."

Jealousy filled Marie's eyes as she put her hands on her slender hips in displeasure. "You and that freak, Nicolai."

"Excuse me?" I hissed through clenched teeth. "You had better watch your tongue."

"Just what are you going to do, Angelina?" She smiled wickedly as her eyes shifted past me.

I was afraid to turn around.

The smile on Marie's face turned upside down. She nodded and walked past me without another glance. My heart beat angrily inside my chest, and I cringed when Tristan's voice filled the room.

"We meet again, my sweet, sweet Angelina."

I was disgusted. "Tristan."

"How funny life is, wouldn't you say?" he chuckled, picking up a long strand of my hair.

"Don't touch me," I warned.

He twirled the strand around his index finger. "Soon you will be begging me to touch you."

"Right…" I rolled my eyes. "Like *that* is ever going to happen."

"Oh, but it is going to happen. You see, I have a little secret, and maybe if you're a good girl, I will share it with you."

"I don't want to share anything with you," I hissed.

He pointed to the wall. "You'll want to share this."

A vision appeared on wall in front of me, like that of a drive-in theater, only this movie was silent. Nicolai's beautiful sunset-colored eyes stared back at me. He had a smile spread across his handsome face. My father was next to him, his hand on Nicolai's broad shoulder. They looked to be chatting like old friends do when they're together. Suddenly, a little girl ran out of the forest and Nicolai bent down with open arms. She jumped into them, followed by a little boy with platinum blond hair.

"It can't be," I said.

"Look at your perfect little family," he said. "Aren't they just so darn cute?"

I pointed at the wall. "What is this?"

"This is their future if you give me what I want."

"And if I don't?"

He smiled. "Then this will be their future." He waved his hand and the vision on the wall changed.

"No," I whispered.

"Yes, I'm afraid so," he replied. "Sad, isn't it?"

The Crimson Moon hung high in the sky, shining its blood-red light down on a small graveyard. The same graveyard my human mother had been buried in. Next to her headstone were four fresh graves.

I shook my head. "This isn't real. You're lying."

"Am I?" he asked. "It's your choice."

Mathias' words replayed through my mind. "*You will have to make a choice…*"

"Give me what I want and your loved ones will live a very long, happy life," Tristan coaxed.

Shuddering, I stared at the graves in front of me. Nicolai, Josiah, Baby Girl, and Baby Boy. They were the names of every single person I loved, including my two unborn children.

The time had come for me to make a choice. A choice that could ultimately lead to the end of the world as I knew it. I didn't know what was worse, letting the ones that meant the world to me die, or letting the world around me die. Mathias was right, this was most certainly going to be the hardest decision I would ever have to make.

Chapter 33
Emotions

Nicolai frowned. He felt as though he couldn't get to Angelina quick enough. So many thoughts ran through his mind and no matter how hard he tried, he just couldn't push them away. What were they doing to her? Was she hurt? Was she even alive? Would he be able to save her?

Bethani nudged him lightly. "Stop it."

Nicolai frowned. "I can't help it. I'm worried sick about her."

"I know," she answered sympathetically, "but she's strong. You know that."

"You're right, but how strong do you have to be before you break?"

A blank expression crossed her face as she fell silent. They continued walking side by side for a moment before Ctephanyi joined them. She pointed towards a cave that could be seen in the distance. "We're almost there."

Nicolai's heart began to race. "In that cave?"

She nodded. "Yes, that's where *they* are."

"They?" Daniel asked, slowing down his pace to join their conversation.

"Yes, *they*," she answered, her white eyes beginning to glow brighter.

He was annoyed by her vagueness. "Okay, can you elaborate as to who *they* actually are?"

She stopped abruptly and stared at him. Her icy eyes made him shudder.

"Daniel, your sister is about to make a choice that will affect all of us. Does it really matter who 'they' are?"

He looked down, feeling somewhat ashamed.

"Mother," Nicolai interjected, "he just wants to know what we're going to be up against."

"What neither of you seem to understand is that regardless of who is with her, it is the choice she is about to make that we must stop. I see into her heart and she is torn. She needs to follow her instincts, but he is playing on her human emotions to win her over."

"He's a trickster! Are we sure she sees through his wicked games?" Nicolai asked.

She nodded. "He now knows what her fears are and what she'll do to protect the ones she loves."

"No, she's smarter than he is," Daniel argued. "She'll figure out what he's up to."

"I wouldn't be so sure," she replied, her lips pursing into a thin red line.

Daniel didn't argue. Angelina was smart, but he also knew every creature felt emotions strong enough to cause all sorts of trouble.

Nicolai quickened his pace. "Well, we just need to get in there and get her out."

Bethani put her small hand on his shoulder. "It's not going to be that easy, my friend—we're being watched." She looked up at the trees and nodded.

He followed her gaze. Sure, enough there were eyes on them from what seemed like everywhere. The vapor demons sat quietly in the trees, watching their every movement.

Daniel caught onto what was being talked about and whispered, "We'll never be able to take on all of them with just the few of us."

"We must try," Bethani said, pulling an arrow out of her quiver slowly.

"She's right," Ctephanyi agreed. "If we don't at least try, then what is the point of coming here in the first place?"

Stephen smiled mischievously. "Well then, I suppose we should show them all what an ass-whooping means, shouldn't we?"

Bethani slowly pulled an arrow out of her quiver and set it in her bow. "I think you're right," she replied with a quick wink.

A big smile spread across Stephen's face. "A wink, huh? See I knew you had the hots for me all along."

"Hots?" She laughed, letting the arrow fly.

Nicolai grinned, "I'm thinking she probably has a case of the 'nots.'"

"You would say something cocky like that, wouldn't you?" Stephen asked.

A high-pitched scream rang out, indicating Bethani's arrow had hit its mark. Suddenly, numerous vapor demons appeared before us.

A challenge had presented itself and Daniel's muscles twitched in anticipation of it. "You ready for this?"

"Oh, you know I am." Nicolai smirked, cracking his knuckles before charging at one of his demon duplicates.

Snow growled and let out a long, vicious howl before leaping into the crowd of demons that were closing in around them. One of the demons let out a shriek, sending the others into a frenzy.

Ctephanyi's eyes brightened. Nicolai, who was standing close to her, grabbed a vapor demon and broke its neck. Appearing out of thin air, the demons swarmed them. They were going to need a miracle to get out of this one.

Chapter 34
Fate

"Some say time goes on forever, you know," Tristan said, smiling wickedly at Angelina, "but most don't get to live forever like we can. All you have to do is agree to be mine."

"All things come to an end," she retorted angrily. "I will never be yours."

"Oh, but my dear, that's where you're wrong."

"I doubt it."

"Doubt what? That time goes on forever or that you'll be mine?" He danced around her. "What you fail to see is that your time with Nicolai is nearing its end."

I felt my face twist into a look of disgust. "Nicolai and I will be together forever, which you cannot and will not change."

He let out a long, hearty laugh. "Why would you want to be with him when I can offer you so much more than he can?"

"And what do you offer me, Tristan? Lies? Deceit?"

He took a step towards me and caressed my cheek. "Angelina, I can offer you the world. Can he offer that to you?"

"What about love, Tristan? Can you offer me that?"

He smirked. "Love? I will make you my Queen, and all that is mine will be yours. You will know no love greater—this I promise you."

"And what would happen to Nicolai?" I questioned.

"I would erase his mind so you wouldn't even be a whisper of a memory; he would have absolutely no recollection of you," he promised.

His words stung. The thought of Nicolai forgetting me and all that we had been through together crushed me. How could one be made to forget the memories that made them who they were—that had brought them so much happiness?

Tristan ran his hand through my hair, "And the little ones you carry within you will grow up to know me as their father."

At that very moment, something clicked in my mind. What was I doing? I was the daughter of Hecate. I had been brought back to this Earth to protect it from evil, and Tristan was 100% pure evil. If I gave into him and his lies, I would have failed everyone and everything that had ever meant anything to me. "No," I whispered.

He leaned in closer to me, "I'm sorry, what did you say?"

"I said *no!*" I repeated, putting my hand on his face, letting the familiar electric current charge through my fingertips and into his chiseled face. His emerald-green eyes stared at me in surprise and he opened his mouth to say something. I lifted a finger to my lips and smiled wickedly. "It's only going to hurt for a moment—this *I* promise."

He struggled to breathe. "You bitch!" he spewed. He frothed from the corners of his mouth.

"Well, that's not a very nice thing to call me, Tristan. You seemed to have forgotten that I have the power to control life and death," I reminded him. With one swift move, I pushed him away. He hit the wall behind him with a deafening thud and slid down. He lay limp and barely breathing. I knew my moment had come. I could finish him. Was it really going to be this easy?

A burning sensation raged through my shoulder and I knew my question had been answered—apparently not. I whipped around and saw Marie staring at me menacingly. I reached up and my hand was met with a sharp pain. Wincing, I realized my hand was pinned to my shoulder by a silver-jeweled dagger.

Marie clapped her hands together in triumph. "Oh, I bet that one hurt!"

Angry tears escaped down my cheeks. Using my free hand, I pulled the dagger out. Vertigo hit me and I fell to my knees. "What…what's wrong with me?" I cried out.

Her lips curled into a wicked smile. "Poison is wonderful, isn't it? Especially when you put it on the tip of your weapons."

My thoughts were drawn to the two miracles growing in my womb. "No," I whispered.

"Don't worry, it's not going to kill you," Marie rolled her eyes, "I'm your best friend, remember? I would never intentionally try to *kill* you."

"No, you would just stab me in the back," I growled in return.

"Nah, I thought the shoulder was much easier," she retorted sarcastically.

A numbing sensation entered my legs and crawled up my spine. Falling to the floor, a harsh realization washed over me—I was paralyzed.

"You know, when we went to prom, that dress looked terrible on you," she quipped.

"Prom?" I struggled to recall the memory. "What does prom have to do with any of this?"

"All eyes were on you as you walked down those steps, like you were the most beautiful girl in the world," she recalled.

Jealousy had reared its ugly head and it was now looking me straight in the face. "What on earth are you talking about?"

"Every single person, including the one I wanted for myself," she continued. "You had him wrapped around your little finger."

"Are you talking about Jeremiah?" I said. "I thought you hated him!"

"Hate? I only acted like I hated him because I couldn't have him. You were the one he wanted, not me."

"Marie, he is like a brother to me," I argued.

"A brother?" She let a cocky laugh. "Try, more like a boyfriend."

"No."

"Yes! He followed you everywhere. In fact, he followed you into the woods, without so much of a care for his own life. All he wanted to do was save you."

"That's what friends do for each other, Marie, they help you." I felt another tear run down my face. "They don't hurt you."

She bent down and wiped the tear from my face with her clammy hand. "Aw, don't feel bad. I'm going to get what was promised to me, and you're going to be given to Tristan, just as I promised him."

One by one, the tears escaped down my damp face. "Please don't do this," I begged.

She stood back up and headed towards the open door. "A promise is a promise. Best friends 'til the end, I say." With that, she disappeared into the opening.

I lay thinking of how my childhood friend had been corrupted by Tristan's evil and jealousy. How had I missed that? Was I so wrapped up in my own problems that I had completely disregarded what was going on with my closest friend?

Sighing, there was one thing I knew for sure, Tristan was going to have one heck of a headache when he woke up.

"Just when I thought this was going to be easy," I muttered.

Nothing in life is easy, my dear," a familiar female voice interrupted. "Nothing at all."

Chapter 35
Diversion

"Watch out!" Bethani yelled, as an arrow whizzed by Daniel's head. He ducked and watched the arrow burrow deep inside her identical demon twin.

"Great shot," Daniel commented, swinging his fist around to hit his own evil self in the face. The figure returned the blow and the copper taste of blood filled his mouth. He sneered and landed a face palm to the figure's septum, causing its bones to shatter.

"Is that all you got?" He smirked, watching the look-alike figure fall to the ground. "Yeah, don't get back up," he warned, "or you'll be joining your little buddies back in hell."

Snow's ferocious growls could be heard nearby, and Daniel shuddered at the thought of her venomous bites. One bite from her meant instant death.

He took a step back as a body flew past him and hit a nearby tree with a deafening thud. He couldn't help but smirk again when he saw the look of sheer enjoyment on Stephen's face. He was such an odd character. Why were vampires always so damn scary looking?

"We have to push forward," Nicolai commanded.

"Where's Ctephanyi?" Bethani called out.

All four of them looked around, but she was nowhere in sight.

There was a look of confusion on his face. "She must've gone ahead without us," he said.

Daniel whistled. "Snow! Come on, girl." There was a loud bark and the sound of something being torn to shreds. "I guess she'll be joining us as soon as she's done with her chew toys."

Stephen cocked an eyebrow.

"What's the matter, Stephen?" Nicolai chuckled. "Oh, that's right, you were her chew toy once."

Stephen rolled his eyes. "Funny."

Bethani giggled. "That it was."

"You guys are so lame," he retorted, strutting towards the opening of the cave.

They all laughed and pushed forward, taking down any demon that stood in their way.

"For some reason, I thought this was going to be harder."

"You're right, Daniel," Nicolai said. "What if…"

"What if what?" Bethani questioned.

"This was just a diversion?"

A hush fell over them. Nicolai was right. These vapor demons weren't quite as threatening as the previous ones they'd fought. These were like mosquitos, simply annoying.

"We need to get inside that cave now!" he ordered. "Something isn't right. My mother has gone missing."

"What if she is the traitor?" Daniel asked.

"Impossible," Nicolai said.

"Why not? She's done it before," he remarked.

Nicolai shook his head in disagreement. "No, she's changed."

"Whatever you say. Stephen, help me clear a path," he said, pushing his weight forward.

They made it to the cave opening and the darkness dared them to come inside.

"Well, what are we waiting for?" he asked, looking at his companions.

Stephen looked at Bethani provocatively. "Let's do this," he said.

She made a gagging face. "I honestly don't want to do anything with you. I thought I had made that pretty clear."

"Hey, a guy can try, right?" he said, disappearing into the cave.

Her sweet voice trailed off as she disappeared into the cave behind him. "He's such a prick."

Nicolai and Daniel stared at each other momentarily.

Daniel grinned. "You ready for this?"

"You better believe it," Nicolai nodded. "Let's go save our girl."

The darkness swallowed them whole as they walked together, shoulder to shoulder. There would be little room for error when they confronted the dangers hidden within the cave.

Chapter 36
Deception

I blinked again to make sure my eyes weren't playing tricks on me. Sure enough, in front of me, stood my mother, Hecate.

Caressing my tear streaked face, she smiled. "Yes, my dear, I'm truly here."

"How are you here?" I croaked, trying to find my voice.

"I saw that Tristan was playing a cruel game, so I thought it was only fair that I broke a few rules myself to even the odds."

My eyes refilled with angry tears. "My best friend has betrayed me. She's helping him."

She frowned. "I know, honey. I know."

I shook my head in disbelief. "I never thought of all people that *she* would turn on me."

Kneeling in front of me, she took my face in her hands. "Listen, my lovely daughter. She's human, and humans are such fickle creatures. They lead with their emotions, and that usually ends up getting them into trouble."

She was right.

"Well." She stood back up and put her hands on her hips. "Let's see how I can help you without actually 'helping' you."

"What do you mean?" I asked curiously.

"Well, I can only do so much without facing my own repercussions, so let's see." She looked around and smirked. "This blade doesn't look right lying here on this table, now does it?"

"Ah!" I knew what she meant. "No, it sure doesn't."

In one swift movement, she knocked the blade off and kicked it towards me.

Though my hands were bound, I found I could quickly snatch up the blade to cut myself free.

"Well, look at that!" Hecate chuckled. "You're free."

I rubbed my bruised wrists and sighed. "Now what?"

"That, my dear, you're going to have to figure out for yourself."

"You have to leave," I stated matter-of-factly.

She smiled and strode over to me gracefully, her long white dress barely making any movement. "I do."

"Thank you," I said. "I don't know what I would've done if you hadn't come along to help me."

"Oh, I'm sure you would've figured out something. You're my daughter, remember?" she replied, kissing me tenderly on the forehead. "Now, go make your mother proud and show this little boy it's not nice to play with our family."

I nodded my head. "I promise, I will."

She kissed me once more before disappearing out the door. I sucked in my breath and looked around. I knew I wouldn't have much time before Marie or Tristan returned. I had to have a plan of some sort if I wanted to get out of this place alive.

Ctephanyi's voice filled the room. "Well, look who I found."

My heart sank a little as I couldn't help but wonder if she too had turned against me like Marie had. "How did you find me?" I asked. "Where are the others?" She took another step towards me and I held up my hand to stop her. "Please, don't come any closer."

"Angelina, no need to be defensive. I'm not here to hurt you."

Laughter halted our conversation as Tristan walked into the room. "Well, what do we have here?!"

Ctephanyi looked back at me, her youthful face twisted into scowl. "I just came to see how you were doing, Tristan."

"I'm doing just dandy, dear," he said, his voice full of sarcasm.

"Really?" she replied, turning back around to face him. "It doesn't quite look like you are."

"Oh, you mean this little battle wound here?" He chuckled, rubbing his chest. "That's nothing compared to what I'm about to do to her. Speaking of, how did you manage to get free?" he questioned, taking a step in my direction.

My hand rose in front of me, and the familiar, warm tingling sensation returned. "Stop," I uttered.

Sheer surprise filled his eyes as he unwillingly did as I asked. "What the hell?"

"Hush." I put my fingers to my lips. "I was having a conversation with my future mother-in-law. It wasn't very nice of you to interrupt us."

He opened his mouth to say something, but no sound came out. Anger replaced the surprised look on his face.

"Ah, if looks could kill, right?" I couldn't help but enjoy a brief moment of satisfaction from my cocky comment.

"Angelina, this is not what you think," Ctephanyi said without hesitation.

I turned my attention to her. "It's not, huh?"

"No, it's not."

"Then why don't you explain what you're doing here."

"It's quite simple, actually—I came to rescue you."

"Oh, I bet you did."

Her icy eyes met my chestnut ones. "It's the truth."

Tristan had an evil grin on his face.

"Is she lying?" I asked. A lump formed inside my throat as he nodded slowly.

"Yes."

"No, Angelina, he's the liar."

I cleared my throat and turned back to face her. "Why would you do this to us again, Ctephanyi? Hell, I'm carrying your grandchildren. Your bloodline!" A realization washed over me. "Oh my god, that's it, isn't it?" My body felt as if it were on fire. "You wanted them for yourself!"

She shook her head defiantly. "No, Angelina, you're wrong. Listen to me…"

"If I wasn't in the picture anymore, then Nicolai could return back underground with you and our children!" I screamed.

"Angelina, calm down, please," she begged.

Tristan clapped in enjoyment behind. "What a splendid show!"

Ignoring his comment, I stared at Ctephanyi in hate. "Nicolai is mine now. These children are ours, and you cannot have them!"

"Angelina, stop. You don't know what you're about to do," she said.

I put my hand over my stomach protectively. "They're mine."

"Honey, I know," she replied calmly. "Now stop this. This is exactly what Tristan wants. He's trying to separate you from your family so he can consume your soul."

My entire body was engulfed in pure hatred. "Liar!" I yelled. "I will not allow you to take them from me!" Electric fire escaped from my fingertips and jolted towards her. "They are mine!" I repeated.

My father's voice suddenly filled the room. "Angelina, no!"

Ctephanyi's eyes were wide with horror. He jumped in front of her, knocking her to the floor. The fiery current hit him hard, and he fell to his knees. A small trickle of blood seeped from the corner of his mouth. "Angelina," he whispered.

The anger left my body just as quickly as it had come. I rushed to his side. "Oh my god, what have I done?!"

He gave me a weak smile. "Angelina, don't blame yourself. Maternal instincts are hard to ignore, and you are half-human, remember? Humans feel emotions stronger than we do. It's just in their nature."

He fell limply into my arms. "No, please don't die," I begged. "Please, I will never forgive myself."

He stared into my eyes lovingly. "I will always be with you," he promised.

"Please," I begged. "I can't lose you again."

He touched my cheek with his clammy hand. "I wasn't able to be there for you while you were growing up."

"Father, please…"

He hushed me. "Angelina…"

Tears streamed down my face. "What?" I whispered, putting my hand over his.

"I am so damn proud of you."

Squeezing his hand, I shook my head to let him know I understood. "I love you, Dad."

The twinkle in his eyes dulled, and his hand went limp against my cheek. "No!" I cried out. "Please come back."

It was too late. He had gone to the same place my human mother had gone, and now they could be together forever. In one sense, that somewhat eased my aching heart, but in another, I knew I had just killed my own father. That was a regret I would never forgive myself for.

Chapter 37
Resentment

The room was quiet. Too quiet, in fact. Lifting my head slowly, I looked around. Nervous eyes watched me intently, fearful of what my reaction was going to be. They had every right to be afraid, because now I understood why humans had so much fear within their hearts. Every species but humans had evil intentions. Humans were weak, and these wicked creatures knew it. I would rid the world of this evil, so not one human had to fear them ever again.

Ctephanyi lowered her eyes in shame. "Angelina," she said, "I'm so sorry."

Her words sent a sharp pain straight to my heart. My jaw tightened as I clenched my teeth together. "Sorry? You're sorry?"

Her eyes were focused on my father's limp body. "Please trust that I'm on your side," she said. "This was not supposed to happen."

My face flushed. "For years, I thought my father was dead," I replied, "and then by some miracle, he is returned to me."

"Angelina…"

"It's your fault he's truly dead."

"No, Angelina, don't say that," she said.

I paced back and forth in front of her. "You did this, Ctephanyi. This is your fault!"

"Oh, Angelina, can you believe this? She truly is the reason your father is dead," Tristan said behind me. "If she wouldn't have betrayed you, your father never would have jumped in front of that kill shot."

"Shut up!" I screamed at him.

Tristan's mouth instantly closed and he struggled to open it.

"I didn't ask for your opinion."

He shot me a dirty look and took a step toward me.

My hand rose in front of him, and he halted, "Maybe you didn't hear me the correctly. I said, I did not ask for your opinion!" I repeated.

Anger filled his eyes once he realized he no longer had control over his body.

Returning my attention back to Ctephanyi, I said, "What I can't wrap my mind around is why my father would save such a traitorous creature from death."

My words had hit their mark. Ctephanyi's eyes shifted to meet mine. "I am no traitor."

"I'm assuming you must miss death." I glared at her, my gaze unfaltering. "Perhaps we should return you there."

She stared at me, her icy white eyes brightened in anger. "Angelina, I do not wish to fight you."

Shrugging, I gave her a deadly look. "I never said I wanted to fight with you. I want to *kill* you."

Everything seemed to move in slow motion. Ctephanyi pointed at me and a white light emerged from the tip of her finger and stopped within inches of my stomach. My hand instantly rose in front of my stomach protectively.

"Do you see that?" a voice whispered.

Confusion washed over me and my eyes darted around the room. Everything had grown eerily still. I looked back at Ctephanyi and it was like she had been frozen in time.

"She was going to murder your unborn children to take back her son," the voice whispered.

"No," my arms wrapped around my stomach protectively, "she can't take them."

"Angelina, look at me," the voice beckoned.

I turned around and Tristan's face was within inches of mine. His emerald-green eyes seemed to peer into my soul. "How did you get free?" I croaked.

He smiled and held up a beautiful necklace that shimmered with runic symbols.

"What is that?"

"Angelina, time is merely a tool that can be altered to our benefit."

I looked down at my stomach, "You stopped her from killing them."

"I love you, and I want you to rule with me—I would never let anyone hurt you."

"I see that now," I whispered.

He held his hand out to me. "Be my Queen. I will protect you and the children—forever."

My human emotions begged me to kill him and return to Nicolai. "Tristan, I…"

"Do not allow your emotions to control you. Emotions are going to be the downfall to all human existence. They are the reason for so many wars, death, and destruction."

He was right. My emotions had done nothing but get the people I loved killed. They had betrayed me time after time. Love was simply an emotion that caused pain and suffering. What good had ever come from it?

"Don't let your humanity destroy you. Let me protect you from this world," he said.

We joined hands, and he smiled. "Together we will rule the world."

"Yes." I nodded. "We will."

He took the necklace and wound it around our hands. Every rune glistened beautifully, casting symbols across the ceiling and bare walls.

An odd sensation filled my body, and I looked up at him in confusion.

"Don't worry, my love. In a moment, we will be bound forever. Our souls forever intertwined so that not even death will be able to separate us."

I closed my eyes and let my mind wander to a place of happiness. Nicolai's beautiful sunset-colored eyes flashed in my head and I frowned. What had I just done?

Chapter 38
Time

Nicolai felt a sharp pain tear through his chest and fell to his knees. What had just happened? He tried to compose himself and remembered that he had only felt that pain once before—when Angelina died.

"Are you okay, old man?" Stephen asked with what Nicolai guessed to be concern in his voice.

He grabbed his chest as another sharp pain sliced through him. "I don't know," he said.

Stephen yelled into the darkness. "Daniel! Hey, we got issues over here, bro."

Nicolai heard Daniel's footsteps hurry towards them. There was concern on his face. "What's wrong?"

Nicolai grabbed his chest in pain. "It's Angelina. We're too late."

Daniel grabbed Nicolai's hand and pulled him back up to his feet. "Suck it up, tough guy," he said. "We have work to do."

"Tristan has the pendant," Nicolai said.

"We have to stop him!" Daniel said in return.

Nicolai's eyes began burned brightly. "He's going to make her his. We don't have much time."

Daniel nodded. "What happened just now? Why were you on the ground?"

Nicolai ignored his question and began to pace back and forth. "I hope we're not too late."

"Nicolai, answer me," Daniel demanded.

Just then, Nicolai heard a loud thud coming from up ahead.

"Hello?" Jeremiah called out.

"Jeremiah! Where have you been?" Stephen asked excitedly. "You missed out on all the fun!"

He limped toward them. "Well, after my exciting capture, I somehow managed to escape. It was almost too easy, actually…" His voice trailed off.

Nicolai put his hand on Jeremiah's shoulder. "It's good to see you're alright. There's much to tell you, but for now, we must hurry."

Jeremiah gave him an inquisitive look.

"We fill you in," he promised.

Stephen put his hand on Nicolai's shoulder and halted him with one forceful squeeze. "Dude, I don't like you. You don't like me, but if Angelina dies again, who the hell am I supposed to pick on? Most certainly not Bethani. She'll shoot an arrow in my ass."

Nicolai peered into the darkness. "Speaking of Bethani, where did she disappear off to?"

Daniel looked around. "I don't know. I thought she was right behind me."

Stephen grinned. "That girl is such a rebel. I like it."

Daniel shook his head. "Instead of thinking with your other head, why don't you focus on the task at hand?"

Nicolai frowned. "If he has the pendant then he's activated it."

Stephen grinned mischievously at Daniel. "Can we not talk in code? I have no idea what the hell you're talking about."

"You just reminded me why I hate vampires," Daniel said.

Stephen held his hand to his mouth and let out a fake gasp. "Why would you hate little ol' us?"

"Stop it, both of you," Nicolai said. "The pendant we speak of controls time. Tristan has the power to start and stop time at any moment he pleases."

"And with Angelina by his side, he will become the deadliest creature to ever walk this Earth," Daniel finished.

Stephen's perfect eyebrow rose in question. "Well, that just doesn't make sense."

"What about that doesn't make sense?" Daniel asked.

"If he activated the pendant and he's messing with time, then why aren't we affected by it?"

Daniel and Nicolai looked at each other. That was a great question.

"He's right, Daniel. If he was using the pendant, we would be frozen in time and wouldn't even be having this conversation," Nicolai replied.

Daniel's eyes grew wide with excitement. "What if…"

"What?" Stephen and Nicolai asked in unison.

"Oh my god, what if it's the babies?" Daniel whispered. "They're a species that's never walked this Earth. Think of the power they must possess. What if

Angelina isn't the key to saving the world, but a locked door? What if they're actually the keys to unlocking her?"

Now Nicolai's full attention was on Daniel. "It's very possible!" he said in excitement.

Daniel's eyes were met with a fiery-orange look of determination. "We can't rule it out."

"It makes sense," Nicolai said. "If the pendant is active, we should not even be having this conversation. That is the only explanation."

"Let's hope we're right," Daniel said.

"Look at you guys hoping for the best," Stephen interjected.

"I've seen crazier things happen. I mean, look at you," Nicolai stated.

Stephen wrinkled up his nose in disgust. "Always such a comedian, aren't you, Nicolai?"

The smirk faded from Nicolai's face as another sharp pain struck him. He steadied himself next to Daniel and rubbed his chest with the palm of his hand.

Stephen gave him a worried look. "You okay, man?"

A weak smile formed on Nicolai's lips. "You worried about me, man?"

He shrugged and dug his hands into his pockets. "No, not at all."

"Yeah, sure." He nodded, an understanding crossing between the two of them.

"If what you guys are saying is true, we don't have much time," Jeremiah interrupted. "Tristan's time on Earth is about to come to an end." He disappeared into the darkness ahead of them.

"Wait!" Nicolai yelled, and disappeared behind him.

"Forget this bromance shit," Stephen mumbled awkwardly. He followed them into the darkness. "I need to kill something."

Chapter 39
His

Ctephanyi stared in silence as the runic symbols engulfed Angelina and Tristan. Their skin shimmered in the golden light that surrounded them.

"Angelina!"

Ctephanyi's eyes darted to the door where Jeremiah appeared, a frantic look on his face. She raised her hand to stop him, but it was too late. He ran towards Angelina at full speed and was flung backwards by an invisible force field. He hit the wall behind him and slumped to the floor.

Ctephanyi sighed and rolled her eyes. "Humans." She scooted over to him and ran her hands over his chest. She could feel the familiar warm sensation of her healing powers leave her body and enter his.

He slowly opened his eyes and stared at her. "What happened?"

"You ran into a wall," she replied, expressionless.

"Really?"

She nodded.

"Why would I do something stupid like that?" he asked, sitting up and quickly answering his own question.

Ctephanyi watched his face run through a multitude of expressions. First, it was a look of surprise, then anger, then sadness, and finally disgust. "You can't do anything to help her at this moment." She put her hand on his cool arm. "She's his."

Tears formed in his eyes. "No," he whispered. "It can't be too late."

She looked down, her own eyes filling with tears. She looked back up, surprised by the human emotion that filled her.

"Mother!" Nicolai's voice entered the room.

A tear of shame fell down her ivory skin. "My boy, oh, my sweet boy, I'm so very sorry."

Nicolai's eyes burned with a fire brighter than Ctephanyi had ever seen. For a moment, she saw Elias in him and shuddered. She knew what her husband had been capable of and what Nicolai could do if he wanted to.

"Angelina!" Daniel called out, entering the room, with Stephen following close behind him.

"She's glowing," Stephen gasped.

"We have to stop this!" Daniel looked around the room frantically.

"Well, don't try running towards them…" Jeremiah frowned, rubbing the back of his head.

"They're being protected by the pendant. It's created a circle of protection around them. They are untouchable," Ctephanyi whispered.

"There has to be a way," Daniel urged.

"Oh, but there is a way," a sweet, girlish voice chirped.

Everyone turned their attention towards the door, including Tristan. They were all surprised by what they saw. Standing beside Bethani was Elias, who happened to be carrying a very angry Marie.

"Marie?" Jeremiah's mouth dropped open. "What in the hell are you doing here?"

Ctephanyi answered for her. "She's a traitor, Jeremiah. She was the one helping Tristan all along."

Anger filled his eyes. "Marie?"

She squirmed in Elias' arms.

Elias grinned, his eyes burning bright red. "Oh, you think so, huh?"

Jeremiah's eyes were full of hurt. "Marie?"

"What?" she shrugged her stiff arms. "It looked like a great opportunity to get what I wanted in life."

He shook his head in disgust. "You were her best friend. How could you?"

She rolled her eyes. "Oh please, she had everything. It was my turn to have it all."

"Do you want to see what happens when you betray a friend?" Bethani asked, her lavender eyes full of mischief.

Marie scowled. "Listen here, you little blonde bitch."

Bethani nodded to Elias and he hurled her forward towards the golden light that surrounded Tristan and Angelina.

"Oh my god, what are you doing?!" Jeremiah watched in horror as Marie's body disintegrated.

A loud explosion rocked the room and they were all thrown backwards against the wall. Dust filled their lungs and they all struggled to come to their senses.

"Nicolai," Ctephanyi croaked. "Elias?"

"I'm here, mother," Nicolai called out from the rubble.

"What the hell just happened?" Stephen growled, his features beginning to change quickly.

"Where's Angelina?" Daniel bellowed from across the room.

"Angelina?" Nicolai said.

The dust from the debris was thick, which made it hard for anyone to see anything. Nicolai stood up and made his way over the debris that covered the room.

"She's over here!" Jeremiah called out from behind him.

"Keep talking, Jer. I can't see you," Nicolai ordered.

"Over here!" Jeremiah yelled again.

Tristan's laughter filled the room. "I told you I would take her from you," he said. Suddenly, Nicolai felt a searing pain rip through his chest. He looked down, his eyes wide with surprise. Sticking out of his chest was a golden dagger.

Tristan smiled, pure evil emanating from his eyes. "Say hello to my father for me once you get to Hell."

Chapter 40
No Pity

I opened my eyes and focused on Tristan and Nicolai. I saw the golden blade sticking out of Nicolai's chest and my heart stopped, right along with his. Lightning soared through my veins as pain and anguish tore at my soul.

What had Tristan done?

What had I done?

I stood up and allowed the vengeful hate to rip apart any emotions and shred any sort of pity I had left for humanity. So, this was what pure hate felt like. It coursed throughout my entire body and I let it consume my soul. I was about to show the world how hateful I could be.

My arms raised unconsciously above my head. Bolts of electricity surged out of my fingertips and through the rocky ceiling above. The beautiful blue sky begged me not to destroy it; however, the time had come for the world to know my sorrow and vengeance.

The clouds began to form and swirl in quiet protest. I blocked out the muffled cries from my companions, as they now meant nothing to me. Every single cell inside my body tingled with angry anticipation. The lightning continued to surge out my fingertips. The sky became pitch black and I called upon the moon. It rose to my beckoning and appeared the same color as the sunset at dusk—a deep crimson. The world as I had known it to be had disappeared and a new world appeared before me. One with fear, loathing, and hate. Every ingredient needed to cause mass wars between the species that inhabited the Earth. It was time. If I felt all these feelings, then the world would feel them too.

"You don't know what you've just done," Ctephanyi croaked.

I lowered my arms and swung around to meet her icy glare. "See, that's where you're wrong."

She watched me, her stare unfaltering, as if to test me. "How so?"

"Angelina, remember…all you have to do is remember," I mocked. "Well, I remember, and now you will see just how powerful I really am."

"Listen to yourself, Angelina. Just listen to yourself," she said.

A small twinge of guilt stabbed at my heart. "I don't need another lecture from you." I turned back around and stared at the crimson-colored moon and mumbled. "Especially because you don't matter to me anymore."

"I hope I still matter to you," a sweet voice chimed in behind me.

Breathing out slowly I said, "Bethani, don't."

"Angelina, you knew this day would come."

"I made a choice."

She nodded. "Yes, you did."

"It was the right choice."

"You don't sound so sure."

I sucked in my breath. "I'm sure."

"You can undo this," she whispered. "You can bring him back."

A warm tear slid down my cheek and shook my head. "No, I can't."

"Yes, you can," she reassured.

I turned to face her. There was promise in her lavender eyes as she smiled and pointed at Nicolai. "You can undo all of this."

My voice trembled. "How?"

"Tristan has the answer," she replied. She pointed to the rune-carved pendant that hung around his neck. "That pendant not only stops time, but also controls it."

"How do you know this, Bethani?" I asked.

"Your mother told me that one day this information would be pertinent…and it was," she replied.

Choking back tears, I asked, "So, I could go back?"

She nodded. "But, you have to want to do it."

I fell silent. The wrath inside of me pulsed through my veins and I cringed at the guilt that had begun to filter in. Could I undo what had been done? Did I really want to?

I felt Bethani's cool breath on the back of my ear. "The path of destruction is not the path you're meant to follow, and you know it."

I swung around and met Bethani's wide eyes with my own. "How do you know?"

"Because I know you, and this isn't who you are," she replied quietly. The look in her eyes were begging the old me to return.

Out of nowhere, a sharp pain tore through my abdomen and I fell to my knees.

"Angelina!" Bethani cried out, falling to my side—her slender arms wrapping around me protectively.

Elias seemed to appear out of nowhere. "We can't let her destroy the world, Bethani. Let her go."

She pulled me closer to her warm body. "No."

"Bethani, I'm warning you…"

"And just what are you going to do, old man?" Stephen snickered from behind him.

Elias responded, his red eyes darkening as he turned around to face Stephen. "I'm doing what must be done to preserve human and nonhuman existence."

Stephen scoffed. "Do you really think that's going to solve anything?" He looked up at the Crimson Moon. "I mean, look at this place."

"If she dies, the world will return to how it once was," he answered matter-of-factly.

Stephen's vampire face twisted its grotesque form. "What about Tristan? Have their souls joined together?"

"No, the ritual wasn't completed," Ctephanyi said.

"So, if you do this, then you just killed not only your future daughter-in-law but your two grandchildren," Stephen said. "Hell, you're a sure win for the grandpa of the year award."

A look of disgust fell over Elias' face. "If you know what is good for you, then you'll keep that ugly mouth of yours shut."

Stephen cocked his head to the side and smiled. "Aw, did I hit a nerve?"

Elias frowned. "I despise your entire race."

"Well, we were never too fond of your race either." Stephen made a disgusted face. "I mean, look at those eyes."

Elias' blood-colored eyes darkened. "You're such a waste, as is this conversation." He turned back around to face Angelina. "I'm sorry I have to do this, my dear, but I must do what is right for all of us."

A warm tear fell down my cheek and I closed my eyes. I was ready for death—I just hoped it was ready for me.

Chapter 41
Risen

Daniel tackled Elias to the ground. "Stop!" he yelled.

I looked around, pulled myself free from Bethani's grasp, and jumped to my feet. I wasn't going down like this. I had come too far to die by the hands of the red-eyed monster that had already tried to kill me once.

"Angelina, run!" Daniel urged as he struggled to keep Elias pinned down.

I looked at Bethani and she nodded. Nothing good was going to come out of me staying here. I glanced at Tristan who was still wearing a shit-eating grin on his face. I felt my own face twist into disgust. Raising my hand, a bright light emerged from my palm and hit him straight in the heart. A look of sheer surprise replaced the grin on his face as he hit the ground.

"That kind of hurt," he sputtered, gripping his chest with one hand.

I reached down and snatched the pendant that dangled from his neck. "I believe I'll take this with me."

He smiled, a trail of blood erupting from the corner of his mouth. "Take it."

I stared at him cautiously. "What?"

"The Crimson Moon has risen," he coughed, and blood splattered across his face.

"Angelina, you need to go now!" Daniel cried out. "I can't hold him for much longer."

"Know this: I will find you," Tristan said.

"I will be waiting," I assured him, hatred in my eyes.

He smiled and closed his eyes. "Until next time."

I scanned the destruction around me and looked at the dirty faces of my companions. They all looked worn and weary.

"You need to go," Bethani whispered.

I looked down and nodded. Escaping out the door, I made my way through the dark cave. Once I reached the opening, I broke into a full sprint through the woods. I felt a twig slice the tender skin on my cheek and cringed. I knew it would heal quickly, but the sting of the cut still hurt.

I ran through the forest for what seemed like hours. My legs ached and I felt the slight twitch of my exhausted muscles begging me to stop. I slowed down and looked around for a safe place to hide for the night. A fallen tree that had created a sort of lean-to caught my eye. I walked over to it with caution. I picked up one of the fallen crimson-covered branches along the ground to cover the openings from any unwanted creatures.

Crawling inside, I leaned my back up against the soft mossy tree. I closed my eyes and breathed in the earthy aroma of the forest. A warm tear fell down my cheek and I sighed. I felt like I was relieving my past, only this time, Nicolai would not be there to save me.

My head rested in my dirty hands and I began to sob quietly. How had it gotten so bad? Was I really that hormonal or perhaps it was just my stubbornness that was preventing me from letting go of the grudge I had been holding against the one man that had been put on this Earth just for me.

I mean, what had he really done that was so wrong? His species surprised me by the love they could carry, and the jealousness they were able to feel. Were those things so bad?

No, they weren't, and now I couldn't take any of it back. I had lost him. Death had taken his soul away from me and I could never get it back—or could I? If I used the pendant and changed one thing, it could potentially alter the way the future was. Was that worth the risk? No, it wasn't.

Suddenly, I knew how to make things right again. I sat straight up and used the back of my hand to wipe my tear-drenched face. I would go to the Underworld and persuade the keeper of souls to give me back my sweet Nicolai. There was only one problem standing in my way, and it was a big one. The keeper of souls just happened to be Tristan's father and I wasn't so sure he was going to be happy to see me.

I closed my eyes again and smiled. My plan unfolded in my head. I would wait for Tristan to find me and then we would go to his father together. I would then persuade Hades to give me back Nicolai's soul in exchange for the pendant. It was a good plan and it had to work.

Chapter 42
Waiting

Tristan's eyes flew open and he threw Daniel off him. His plan had worked perfectly. Angelina had the pendant and he would be able to track her easily. He jumped up and dusted himself off.

"You're never going to win her heart," Ctephanyi muttered from the rubble.

"Always such a pessimist, aren't you?" he replied, a smirk gracing his bloody face.

"She's right, you know," Bethany chimed in. "Angelina's heart belongs to Nicolai."

He shot her a dirty look. "We shall see about that."

"There will be no seeing about anything," Daniel called out gruffly from the floor. "My sister is going to kill you."

Tristan laughed. "Please humor me, Daniel. Why do you think your sister is going to kill me when I have the one thing she wants the most?"

Daniel looked at him in confusion. "What are you talking about?"

Tristan bent down and pulled the gold dagger out of Nicolai's chest. "You see this?" he asked. "This dagger is holding Nicolai's soul."

"It exists?" Elias breathed.

Tristan smiled. "Why yes, my dear Elias, it does."

"What exists?" Daniel questioned, staring at the gold dagger that shimmered underneath the crimson moonlight.

"This dagger here just happens to be enchanted with a very powerful spell that only a keeper of the Underworld can cast."

"Your father," Ctephanyi whispered.

Tristan smiled wickedly. "You bet! It was a gift for just in case things got…difficult."

Daniel grinned. "Your father was right. Things are going to get very difficult for you."

Tristan twirled the dagger around in his hand. "Is that so?"

"Angelina wasn't meant for you," Ctephanyi replied angrily. "She was meant for my son."

He let out a snarky laugh. "Oh, you mean that pile of emptiness on the floor?"

Ctephanyi's eyes grew bright white instantly and she stood up. "That pile of emptiness on the floor is my son."

"Yeah, and he's dead."

The tension in the air was heavy. Tristan knew Ctephanyi wanted to rip him apart but wouldn't dare do so because he held the one thing that could bring him back. He let out a loud roar of laughter. "What's the matter, Ctephanyi? Why so speechless?"

She stared at him, pure hatred emanating from her icy white glare. "You will get yours."

Bethani touched Ctephanyi's arm tenderly. "Now is not the time."

Ctephanyi's gaze was unmoving. "When will it be time?"

She smiled sweetly. "Soon."

Ctephanyi nodded. "Fine, but we shall see each other again soon."

Smiling, he looked at her. "Promise?"

Returning his smile, she motioned for her companions to head toward the door. "You can bet your life on it."

Daniel crossed his arms in defiance. "So, we're leaving? Just like that?"

Ctephanyi nodded. "Yes, Daniel. Fear not, we shall see him again soon."

"Well, why can't we just finish it right now?"

"Yeah? Why can't we finish it right now?" Jeremiah demanded.

Ctephanyi narrowed her eyes sternly. "Because now is not the time."

The two men looked at each other in disappointment.

"Now go, both of you," she demanded, pointing towards the door.

With one final huff, they trudged out the doorway, followed by Bethani and Elias. Ctephanyi turned her attention once more on Tristan. "The next time we meet, you will not be so lucky."

Tristan's green eyes twinkled. "Perhaps it is you who won't be so lucky."

Ctephanyi's face twisted into a look of disgust. "We shall see."

Tristan watched her walk out the door in silence. "Oh, yes, we sure will."

Chapter 43
Emptiness

A pleasant voice whispered, "Angelina, it's time to wake up."

"Just a few more minutes," I asked sleepily.

"Angelina, you need to open your eyes," the voice whispered again.

"But, I'm so tired," I begged.

In a much sterner tone the voice called out. "You need to wake up now."

I wiped the sleep from my eyes. "Fine."

The sound of rustling leaves nearby caught my attention and I was suddenly wide awake. My heart raced as I peeked out my makeshift door. Covering my mouth in horror, I choked down the bile that rose instantly. Mathias' bloody head was propped outside, and in one colorless eye was the golden dagger that had killed my beloved Nicolai, along with a bloody letter. His other eye stared at me in desperation. A rogue tear escaped down my cheek as I tried to calm myself down. Taking a deep breath, I wiped away the tear and listened. The frail, weathered leaves rustled across the ground while the Cerulean Warbler sang its sweet tune nearby. I slowed my breathing and concentrated harder, listening for anything out of the ordinary. Just then, I heard it. The cracking of a tree branch under the weight of something heavy. My hand trembled slightly as I saw a humanoid creature fleeing from the forest.

"I'm coming for you," I whispered with promise. Careful not to make any noise, I pulled myself free from my makeshift home. Scrambling to my feet, I reached over and snatched the letter off the golden dagger that twinkled under the midmorning sun. I unfolded it carefully and read:

My dearest Angelina,

The time for our union was ruined by your dear friends. However, it shall happen soon. There are still loose ends that need to be taken care of. What stopped our past from being together in the present will not follow us into the future. The dagger is yours. Consider it a wedding gift. My father will be waiting for you.

Tristan

Was this some sort of sick joke? Hatred and anger crept into my heart as I crumbled up the piece of paper and threw it into the woods. I would make him pay for all the pain and suffering he had caused to the people that meant the most to me.

This was what my life had become. Death and destruction. I was no longer the innocent girl full of wonder about the world; in fact, I was the complete opposite. I hated the world and everything it possessed. Everything I loved had been ripped away from me, taken by the world and the monsters that hid within it.

I yanked the dagger out of Mathias, wiping the bloody blade across my jeans. I secured it carefully at my side and looked back at my bloody friend. I stared into his colorless eye and wondered if he would become one of the many stars in the night sky to help watch over me. The idea of him being with my mother and father gave me some sort of quiet peace. "Don't worry, my friend," I whispered, "I will avenge your death."

A whisper carried through the wind and kissed my ears. *"A choice must be made."*

I closed my eyes and breathed in the sweet scent of the Earth. "I know," I whispered back.

I knew it was time to make things right. Time healed all wounds, including those that were inflicted by those closest to you. The world would heal, and in the end, all would be right once again.

Smirking, I faced my path. "Ready or not, here I come," I breathed into the wind. I knew it would find him and deliver its message. The Earth was dying and I was the only one that could save it.

Chapter 44
Death's End

Daniel pushed past Jeremiah. "You know Angelina's going to try and bring Nicolai's soul back, and there's only one way to do that."

Ctephanyi nodded. "Yes, by going to speak with Hades."

Jeremiah nodded as well. "We won't be able to stop her."

"Then we should help her," Bethani chimed in sweetly.

"Where is she?" Jeremiah asked.

"In the Underworld," Daniel replied.

"Can we even follow her into the Underworld?" Jeremiah questioned, looking back at Ctephanyi. "Isn't that like…Hell?"

"There's a way," Daniel said. "Ctephanyi can get us there."

"It's too risky," she replied quietly.

Jeremiah stopped, shock on his face. "Too risky? Are you kidding me? Everything we've done today is risky!" he pointed out.

"This is a"—Ctephanyi put a finger to her lips and was thoughtful—"different kind of risky."

"What's that supposed to mean?" Daniel asked gruffly.

She turned her attention to Daniel. "When you think of the term Underworld, what do you think of?"

"Hell, of course," he replied.

"And by saying the word 'Hell,' you're referring to a place full of demons and fires for an eternity?" she quizzed.

He shrugged. "Well, yeah."

She laughed. "Well, ignore what you know and let me enlighten you."

"Please do," Daniel replied.

"You see, the Underworld was one of the first things created on Earth. The Gods knew that with good, evil always followed. However, some evil is born darker than others. After much deliberation, the Gods decided to create a place for only those that have committed the most unthinkable crimes against humanity.

Stephen looked amused. "So, no fire, no brimstone?"

"Only on the level above it," she said.

"So, what's so bad about this place then? You're making 'spending a life of eternity in torture and agony' sound like a walk in the park. How could it possibly be worse than Hell?"

Ctephanyi had a distant look in her eyes. "Your soul is lost forever. You must spend an eternity battling yourself. Some say that's the worst fate a person could receive."

"Well, it doesn't sound so bad to me," Stephen said. "In fact, I've probably been to worse places."

She laughed. "We shall see."

"We're all alive, right?" Jeremiah said. "So, how can it be a threat to us?"

"The Keepers of the Underworld are always looking for fresh souls. It's quite possible to lose your soul in such a place, and once you lose it, you can never come back to the land of the living."

"So, what you're basically saying is that because we're alive, we could potentially lose our souls and die?" Jeremiah asked.

"Because you are alive, you could indeed lose your soul, but you would not simply die." Bethani's sweet voice rose behind them. "You become your worst, most lonely self. Always searching for something you would never find."

"Well that doesn't sound so bad. Almost vacation-like for me," Stephen said.

Bethani looked disgusted. Scowling, she pushed passed him. "You would say that."

Confused, he replied. "Touchy subject, I see."

Without another word, she walked ahead of them briskly.

"What's her problem?" he asked turning, back towards Ctephanyi.

"You're not used to seeing such negativity from her, are you?" Ctephanyi said.

Stephen tried to shrug off how Bethani's sour reply had affected him. "I guess not."

"When the time is right, she will tell you."

"Tell me what?" he asked.

"How she lost her mother to the Underworld," Ctephanyi answered, walking past him.

Stephen's eyes lit up. "So, her mother's soul…"

Elias nodded. "Bethani was never able to find it," he said.

Stephen's face soured into a sullen expression. "This is dumb," he said.

"I see you're not used to feeling so sympathetic towards another creature," Elias remarked. "We're all experiencing new feelings right now."

Stephen didn't say a word; instead, he walked briskly to try to catch up with Bethani. Elias shook his head and gave Daniel a nod. "He'll be alright."

Daniel laughed. "Maybe feeling something other than being an asshole will be good for him."

Elias chuckled right along with him. "Alright, we should get going."

Ctephanyi tried to hide the smile that had begun to form on her face. "You two…"

"Shall we see if we can go save a couple of souls?" Jeremiah asked.

"If we're all in agreement, and you understand the risks involved, then yes," Ctephanyi said.

Jeremiah's face lit up with excitement. "These Keepers of the Underworld have no idea what they're dealing with."

Ctephanyi gave him a tight-lipped smile as she walked past him slowly. "Jeremiah, dear, it's you that has no idea what you're going to be dealing with," she uttered quietly.

Together, as a group, they followed Ctephanyi to an unknown place.

Stephen suddenly slowed his pace. "So, the only way to do this is through the Underworld?"

"Are you scared?" Daniel joked.

Bethani giggled. "Yeah, what happened to that strong, cocky vampire we've all come to enjoy so much?"

"I've just heard some stories…that's all."

Daniel stopped, an amused expression on his face. "You *really* are scared?"

"Listen, all I'm saying is, many of my vampire brethren have adventured to this terrible place only to never return."

"Well, we're not vampires," Daniel replied. "Now come on, let's get going."

Together, with Stephen a short distance behind, they followed Ctephanyi to this dangerous, unknown place.

Chapter 45
The Beginning of the End

The breeze kissed Tristan with Angelina's message and he smiled. His plan had worked. She was coming for him. The time had come for him to open the Gateway to the Underworld, so he could pull her in and claim her soul. Together they would rule both the surface world and the Underworld. His father was going to be very pleased by this.

He reached into his pocket and pulled out a quarter-sized gold coin. He ran his long fingers over the interlocking triangles on the face of it. An upside-down scythe graced the bottom of each of the triangles. His father had given it to him as a gift the day he decided to rule the world of the living. The coin held immense power and was his most prized possession—except for Angelina, who he couldn't quite call his yet.

The coin was passed down to every first-born son in his bloodline. Those who inherited were given extreme power but had to follow very strict rules. One of the most important rules being that it could never leave your side. Without it, you were trapped in the Underworld for all eternity.

The coin was also a key to opening a portal from the realm of the living to that of the dead. This allowed Tristan to pass freely between the two as he wished. However, another important rule was he had to keep his trips to the surface as short as possible. The coin was made to reap souls and take away all that is living. Every time his feet touched the surface, the coin would extract life out of the Earth—killing it slowly.

Tristan was surprised when his father had passed the coin on to him. With thoughts of Angelina in mind, he had begged his father to give him the coin. There had been so much anger and animosity between them because his father had refused every single time. Then, one day out of the blue, his father had handed him the coin.

No hesitation, no argument, not even so much as a word. Tristan never asked why, he just closed his hand around it and smiled.

He rubbed the coin between his thumb and index finger. A soft glow surrounded it and he set it down in the cluster of dead leaves. The breeze grew still and dark, swirly clouds formed in front of him. The Earth shuddered, and the portal between the World and the Underworld opened. Tristan smiled. He knew Angelina would follow him and risk her soul for love.

Tristan picked up a handful of dead leaves and crushed them in his hands. "Tell them I'll be waiting for them," he whispered.

He threw the pieces into the air. The breeze caught them and carried them off. Trap after trap. He knew the other adventurers would follow Angelina to the Underworld. They would be a present for his father, who would appreciate some new, healthy souls for his collection. That would be a fair gift for allowing him to pursue his heart's desire.

He looked around the crimson-colored forest and breathed in its earthy scent. It was hard to believe that this was all going to be his. Once he won over Angelina's soul, he would work on her heart and together they would rule the world. He knew the great power she possessed. He had seen it in her soul the first time he had met her in the forest with her mother and brother. It was at that very moment he knew she was meant for him. Together they were going to be unstoppable.

Smiling, he breathed out slowly. This was a good place to wait for them. They would find the portal and go through it, assuming he was already inside. Once they were all through it, he would shut the portal, locking them all in the Underworld forever. This was his playground, and they would have to play by his rules.

His smile grew bigger and he chuckled to himself. "Soon Angelina, you'll be mine."

Chapter 46
All That Matters

The air grew stagnant, and the earth around me seemed to be dying at an alarming rate. I sensed Tristan nearby, and a feeling of dread crept into my heart. I was sure he had opened a rift between the two worlds.

Shuddering at the feeling, I pushed away memories of my own death. A light breeze ruffled my hair carelessly. Fragments of dried leaves grazed my cheek softly as they flew by.

Up ahead, a dark cloud swirled between two large oak trees. As I got closer, I noticed everything around the vortex had died. The crimson moss that had been wrapped around the trunks of the trees was black and ashy. The ruby-red and yellow autumn leaves were brown and broken. The wildlife had scattered, which left an eerie silence. It sent a shiver up my spine. Life did not like Death, but Death sure did love Life. It held onto life, taking in its breath and desiring to once again live amongst all that walked the world.

The dark cloud swirled in front of me. This portal would take me to Nicolai. There were going to be many risks, especially because my soul had crossed through the portal before. The Keeper had seen that my soul was special, and I was sure he would love to add it to his collection. The only thing that could potentially stop him was my mother. She had been the Goddess that had sentenced him to the Underworld for his crimes. There were still rules he had to follow. Even though I was born human, my real mother's power ran through me, and he would know that.

The portal whispered my name and promised me no harm. It lied to me and told me there was nothing to be afraid of. My heart raced and I slowly started to talk myself out of it.

What good would come of me going there? Would I even survive? What if I lost my soul? What if I couldn't bring Nicolai back?

Suddenly, I felt little flutter inside my stomach and smiled. A vision of Nicolai as a father entered my mind. What a great dad he would be. A tear slid down my cheek. I couldn't give up on him. I needed him, and so did my unborn children.

Taking a step inside, I was immediately sucked into the darkness. It felt cold and unforgiving. The darkness closed in around me, and for a brief moment, I thought I'd gone blind. Thankfully, my eyes adjusted quickly. The hallway in front of me was dim, but somewhat illuminated by the soft glow of rusty and old iron lanterns. The portal was still open, and though I wanted to turn around, I couldn't. Nicolai was down here somewhere, and I hoped Tristan was down here too.

Chapter 47
Irony

I followed the hallway as far as it would take me until I came to two doors. One was red and the other was black. "Choices?" I muttered to myself. "How ironic."

"But is it?" a deep voice asked.

Suddenly, I found myself staring into a set of deep, emerald-green eyes.

"It is," I replied.

His jet-black hair fell into his eyes slightly. "Then perhaps you should see what is on the other side of these doors." He smiled.

"What's on the other side?" I asked, raising my brow.

"One door is your deepest desire."

"And the other?"

"Is your deepest regret."

I shook my head, confused. "Well, that doesn't make sense."

"Oh, but it does, my dear," he replied.

"Desire and regret? I mean, wouldn't someone automatically choose what they desire over what they regret?" I questioned.

"Most do," he stated matter-of-factly.

"What about those who don't?"

"Maybe you should find out," he said.

Staring at him, I debated on which door to choose. "What if what I desire and what I regret are the same thing?"

He looked at me, surprised. "Well, I am not quite certain I have experienced that dilemma before."

I returned his surprise. "Really?"

He nodded. "Most of the souls that come here are already damned. Either way you look at it, they are going to face something terrible. Whether it be the thing they desire the most that they can never have, or the one regret they will have to live repeatedly."

I shuddered. "Well, when you put it that way, they both sound terrible."

"It's different for each person. The people that belong here, they experience their own personal hell regardless of which door they choose; however, the people that don't belong here"—he smiled again—"their outcome sometimes differs."

I smiled back. "I understand."

He bowed before me. "Choose a door and choose it wisely."

Which door to choose? I could choose what I desired and gamble that everything would turn out exactly as I'd hoped, or I could choose regret and go back to fix things.

"May I give you one piece of advice?" he asked, his green eyes beckoning me to say yes.

I nodded. "Sure. A little advice never hurt anybody, right?"

He nodded in return, a slight smile on his face. "Love is worth fighting for. If you give up on it, it will eat you alive and you'll end up here. You'll end up alone and soulless. Fight for love, fight for it until your soul has no other reason but to cross the boundaries of life and death to win." He pointed towards the doors in front of me adding. "Only true love can do that, you know."

"Do what?"

"Cross the boundaries of both worlds without the coin."

"Can I ask you a question?" I asked quietly.

"Of course."

I looked up at him, hesitation in my voice. "Do you know who I am?"

He stared at me intently.

"I'm sorry, I didn't mean…"

"No," he replied calmly. "It's just, you look so much like her."

"Who?"

"Your mother, Hecate."

I felt myself begin to tense up. "So, you do know who I am."

"There's no need to be on the defense, my dear. There are rules here that I must follow per the Gods."

"So, you aren't going to try and take my soul?"

He laughed. "I couldn't take it from you if you tried to give it to me."

Feeling somewhat rejected, I asked, "Why not?"

He laughed again and pointed to the doors in front of us. "Choose wisely." With a wink, he disappeared, leaving me utterly confused. First, why couldn't he touch my soul? Second, why was he trying to help me? Lastly, why feel rejected that he couldn't take my soul?

Whatever, I thought, throwing my hands up.

Choose wisely, choose wisely, that's all I'd heard lately. Everything I did was a choice. Regret or Desire. One choice. I could go back and fix things, but what if I couldn't fix them? If I chose desire, I could have it all. There was no having to fix things, no having to wonder if it was going to be worth it.

Closing my eyes, I tried to clear my mind. Any other normal eighteen-year-old girl wouldn't have such complicated problems. I mean, what I wouldn't give for my worst worry to be which dress I was going to wear on a hot date—but I wasn't normal. A memory of Cole flashed through my mind. I thought about how animals were made of pure love and held no regrets. They simply gave to the world around them, asking for nothing in return. Cole had given up his life for my happiness and maybe that's exactly what I needed to do. Give up my happiness for his life. That was it.

I turned towards the black door and, without hesitation, opened it, whispering to anything that would listen. "Nicolai, I'm coming."

Chapter 48
Boundaries

"We all need to be on the same page," Daniel stated.

"So, then we're in agreement?" Jeremiah nodded. "You'll stay here while I go into the portal."

Daniel crossed his arms. "Absolutely not, that's my sister. I'm going."

"Someone has to stay here," Jeremiah demanded angrily. "What if the portal closes? Who is going to reopen it?"

"Well, then I should stay behind," Ctephanyi interjected.

"How is it that you're the only one that can open it anyways?" Jeremiah asked.

She pulled a gold coin from the leather wristlet on around her wrist. "With this."

Daniel had heard about the coin that could open the portal between the two worlds. "Where did you get that coin?" he asked. "I thought the coin was in the hands of the Keeper."

"There are, in fact, *two* gold coins, Daniel; however, that's a story for another time," she replied.

Elias put a protective arm around his wife's waist. "I will stay here with you, my love."

"Now wait a minute," Daniel frowned. "I don't know how I feel about that."

Bethani put her hand on his shoulder. "We have no choice but to trust them."

"You have nothing to fear, Daniel. We love her just as much as you do," Ctephanyi confirmed.

He shrugged Bethani's arm off him. "I highly doubt that."

"Daniel, wait," Elias said.

"I'm not waiting for anything." With that, he was gone.

Bethani sighed and went after him.

Jeremiah stood quietly by.

"Jeremiah, you are linked to our kind," Elias said. "You know we are being honest."

"You're sure Ctephanyi can reopen the portal?" he asked.

"If she has the coin, then yes, I'm certain," Elias replied.

"Then Daniel, Bethani, Stephen, and I will go," Jeremiah said.

"Oh, you just wait one minute," Stephen called out, irritated. "Don't you go making choices for me, got it, boy?"

Jeremiah puffed out his chest and flexed his muscles. "Who are you calling a boy?"

"Do you see me looking at anyone else right now?"

"Why don't you show us the ugly face you got hidden underneath that human mask?" Jeremiah suggested.

Stephen laughed. "You better watch yourself there, boy. You may make me actually experience what you would call 'anger.'"

Bethani jumped in between them. "You two cannot do this right now!"

They both stopped and stood quietly in front of her.

She pointed to the black swirling vortex ahead of them. "My best friend is in there."

"Wait," Jeremiah interjected. "Is that it?"

"It's already open!" Daniel exclaimed.

Ctephanyi eyed the area cautiously. "That means Tristan is either here, or inside it."

"I'm ready for him," Daniel said, walking toward it.

"Stop," Ctephanyi commanded. "Bethani is right, no more fighting. The darkness will play with your soul. It's easier for the Keeper to reap your soul if you're surrounded by negative thoughts."

Stephen shoved his hands into his pockets and looked down. "Ctephanyi knows what she's talking about. I've heard the stories of the Underworld. They're not of the pleasant kind."

"Aren't vampires supposed to be soulless?" Jeremiah asked.

"Nobody knows the answer to that question, Jeremiah," Stephen replied. "Not even me."

"Maybe we'll find out," he said.

For a moment, Stephen didn't say anything. Finally, he looked up and smiled. "I don't think I even want to know. Souls get you into all kinds of trouble. Hell, Angelina certainly knows that."

His words hit Jeremiah like a hot pan to the face. "That's not funny one bit. At least she knows what 'real' emotions feel like," he said. "Could you imagine a world without love? No pain, no fear, no nothing? Oh, that's your life every day. Sorry, bro."

Stephen looked at the portal. "Those are the emotions I blame for what's wrong with the world today. Those are the key drivers to why there are wars, famine, and worse."

"No, Stephen, it's you who are wrong," Bethani said, a serious tone in her voice. "It's choices that are to blame for what goes on in the world around us, not feelings or emotions."

"Yeah," he muttered. "Emotionally-driven choices."

Daniel shook his head. "This conversation is getting us nowhere. We need to get in there and get Angelina."

Jeremiah pointed to Daniel, Bethani, and Stephen. "Then it's decided, you three are coming with me. Ctephanyi and Elias will stay here with Snow and keep the portal open."

They all nodded in agreement. Snow barked to show her enthusiasm. The four of them stood arm in arm in front of the portal.

"Keep a close eye on your soul." Stephen laughed.

"Easy for you to say." Jeremiah chuckled. "My bet is that you don't have one."

With that, they stepped into the portal, each one hoping they didn't come face to face with their own personal hell.

Chapter 49
Mirrored

A tear fell down my cheek as I opened my eyes and realized I was back at the bed and breakfast. The warm smell of cinnamon apples filled my nose and I ran to the kitchen to see my mother standing there, humming *Brown Eyed Girl*.

"Mom," I croaked.

"Oh, for heaven's sake, Angelina!" She wiped her hands on her apron and walked over to me, wiping away my tears. "Why on earth are you crying?"

"Mom, you're…you're okay," I managed to say through the tears.

"Of course, I am okay. Why wouldn't I be?" she asked, confused.

"Mom, you can't ever leave me," I begged. "Please, don't ever leave me."

The bell over the front door chimed and she smiled. "We have guests."

I nodded. "Mom, I'm so sorry."

She untied her apron and used the corner of it to wipe away one last tear. "For what, hun?"

"For not being grateful for our ordinary lifestyle and how incredibly ordinary I was."

She laughed and wrapped her arms around me tenderly. "Angelina, stop this nonsense, you silly girl."

A male voice cleared his throat from outside the door, and my mother excused herself. I stood there for a moment, dumbfounded by what was happening to me. I had chosen regret. There were so many things I had come to regret recently, and Hades had given me the opportunity to fix them all.

"Angelina, can you check this young man in?" My mother's voice called out from the front desk.

"Coming," I answered, a new bounce in my step. I pushed past the door that separated the two rooms and caught my breath—it was Nicolai.

"This good-looking fella right here says he would like a room for the night." She grinned happily at me.

"Mom…" I warned.

She threw her hands into the air. "What? I'm just saying, it's nice to see a good-looking boy in here who would like to stay with us, and I would like my very single daughter to check him in."

"Oh my god, Mom!" I laughed, and before berating her, I decided a hug would do instead.

"What's that for?" she asked, surprised by my reaction.

"That's because you have always known what was best for me." I smiled. "Always."

She stared at me lovingly. "What on earth has come over you?"

"Maybe I just realized a few things," I said.

She smiled, accepting the answer I had given her. "Well, in that case, you keep on realizing."

"I plan on it," I promised.

With her looking as if she was about to cry, I reminded her about her apples. She smiled and walked back into the kitchen.

I turned back towards the charming man that was casually leaning up against the counter.

"Isn't this a quaint little bed and breakfast?" he complimented.

"I think so," I teased.

"So, what do you do around here for fun?"

"You," I laughed.

He looked at me in surprise. "Excuse me?"

"Like you haven't heard that joke before," I laughed.

In a serious tone, he responded, "No, I haven't heard that joke before."

Was he an alien? "It's me, Angelina."

"Okay and…"

That's when it hit me. I was experiencing my own personal hell. I thought back and remembered how I had wished I had never met Nicolai. If I had never met him then none of this would've ever happened. That was my regret, and I was now coming face to face with it. A life with him never knowing who I was, but me always knowing him. That was the worst fate that could have been bestowed upon me.

Chapter 50
Self-worth

Jeremiah let his eyes adjust to the darkness that surrounded them. "Is everyone okay?"

"Yeah," Daniel answered gruffly.

"I'm fine," Bethani said, her sweet tone echoing down the hallway in front of them.

"How about you, vampire?" Jeremiah asked, looking around the room.

"I'm just dandy."

He rolled his eyes. "I suppose that's good."

"This is it?" Daniel asked, walking down the hallway.

Stephen nodded. "Yep."

"No fire," he stated.

He shook his head. "Nope, it's worse than fire."

They walked down the hall in silence, each one wondering how bad of a place it really was. They stopped in front of the two doors.

"One red and one black," Jeremiah noted.

"Welcome," a male voice replied behind them.

Hades stood before them.

"You're Tristan's father," Daniel confirmed.

Hades nodded. "You would be correct."

They all looked at each other in confusion. "Then why aren't you attacking us?"

"The Gods have set rules that I must follow. It is not my place to meddle with fate," he answered simply.

Bethani looked at Stephen in suspicion and turned back to the green-eyed man in front of her. "I assume you know what your son has been up to?"

"One question at a time, please." he looked at Stephen. "To answer yours, my job is to bring in new souls and give them the fate they so deserve."

Bethani stopped him short. "And the answer to my question?"

"And to answer your question, my dear, yes, I do know what Tristan is doing."

"You agree with him?" she asked.

He simply replied, "My son is very clever. I've taught him well."

Stephen looked at the despair that crossed Bethani's face and felt a stab in his cold heart.

"Do you know where her mother's soul is?" he said, the words falling right out of his mouth.

They all looked at Stephen in utter surprise.

A tear fell down Bethani's cheek. Startled at herself, she cried out, "What's this?"

Stephen used his thumb to wipe the tear gently from her face. "It's called a tear."

She pushed his hand away. "Don't touch me."

Hades put his large hand on Bethani's shoulder and squeezed it lightly. "I know where your mother's soul is."

She looked up at him, her big lavender eyes full of tears. "Can I save her?"

He shook his head. "Not today."

She didn't understand. "Not today?"

His eyes met hers. "That's not why you're here."

"No, but…"

"Stay true to the course in front of you, Bethani," he ordered.

She nodded. "But I can come back for her?"

He smiled and let go of her shoulder. "Of course you can."

She smiled in return and looked at the doors. "Which one did Angelina go in?"

"I cannot tell you that. I can only tell you one of them is for Desire, and the other is for Regret," he replied.

Jeremiah studied each of the doors. "Which one would she choose?"

"If I know Angelina, she'd choose Regret," Stephen scoffed. "That girl would change the world in any way, shape, or form if she could."

They all stared at him.

"What?" he asked. "Stop looking at me like that."

Daniel playfully slapped Stephen on the back. "No, you're right!"

"That's exactly what she would do," Jeremiah laughed.

Bethani smiled and opened the door. "Well, then Regret it is."

They all looked at the man standing in front of the door. How could the keeper of something so heartless be so helpful?

Only he knew the answer to that one.

Chapter 51
One Final Choice

Tristan watched Ctephanyi from behind a crimson-covered tree. He smiled as the moss began to shrivel up and flake off. He loved the fact that he controlled the life of so many of the creatures around him. His eyes returned to the lovely couple waiting outside the portal. He smiled at the surprise he had in store for them.

"Mother?" a voice called out from the trees.

Ctephanyi's head perked up. "Nicolai?"

"It's a trick," Elias said, pulling her closer to him.

"No, it can't be," she replied.

"Mother, help me!" the voice cried out in pain.

"Elias, we have to help him!" she said, pulling free of his grasp.

"Ctephanyi, no!" Elias called out after her.

Tristan grinned as they ran towards the voice. He stepped out quietly from behind the tree and walked steadily towards the portal. He would wait for them there, and then snatch the coin from Ctephanyi.

An old woman stepped out from behind a nearby oak tree. "Stop right there," she ordered.

Surprised by her appearance, he stopped in his tracks. "And you would be?"

"Angelina's grandmother," she said.

"You're still alive?"

She put her hands on her hips. "I may be old, but I'm not dead."

"How did I miss this tidbit of information?"

"I moved away for a while," she replied. "I was becoming too obvious."

Tristan laughed. "Ah, always hiding from the humans."

She glared at him. "My granddaughter is in there, and I fully expect her back."

He pushed passed her. "Move out of my way, old lady."

She continued glaring at him as he disappeared inside the portal. The ground trembled angrily as it began to close.

Ctephanyi came running toward them. "What are you doing, you fool?"

"He came for your coin!" she yelled.

"Close the portal!" Elias called out from behind his wife.

Ctephanyi rubbed the coin between her fingers and the portal closed.

Elias comforted his wife. "It's going to be okay."

"If my granddaughter's friends know anything about her, they'll know she'll pick the door to Regrets."

Ctephanyi nodded in agreement. "You're right."

"We have to give them time."

"What about Tristan?" Elias asked, looking at the spot where the portal had been.

The old woman looked at him and pursed her lips together. "He will be dealt with."

Ctephanyi stood up and watched the old woman intently. "How do you know all this?"

"I have the gift of sight," she said. "Or perhaps I should say curse."

"As do I, but I cannot see what you claim."

"I see past what you see, Ctephanyi." The old woman leaned up against a nearby tree. "I see through life and death."

Elias looked up at the Crimson Moon. "How long do we wait?"

"We'll know when the time is right," she answered.

Chapter 52
Crazy

"Cat got your tongue?" Nicolai asked, lightly tapping his fingers against the counter.

My chin quivered. "Oh, I'm sorry." I smiled, grabbed a pen, and opened the reservation book.

He put his hand over mine. "Are you okay?"

Looking into his eyes, I tried to talk, but no sound came out.

"Angelina!"

I spun around to see Jeremiah running down the stairs towards me. "What are you doing here?!"

"Angelina, you're okay!" he cried out, wrapping his strong arms around me.

"Where are the others?" I asked, looking up the stairs.

"They're coming," he promised.

Sure enough, Bethani and Daniel came running down the stairs to meet us.

I looked at them and shook my head. "You shouldn't have followed me here."

Daniel pulled me in for a big bear hug. "Since when do any of us ever listen to you?"

"Careful now." I pointed towards my tiny baby bump.

Nicolai looked down and smiled. "Expecting, I see."

Bethani looked at him in confusion. "Yes, with your children."

"Bethani, no." I put my hand on her arm and she looked at me, confusion in her lavender eyes.

She pushed past me and grabbed Nicolai by his shoulders. "This is Angelina, and don't you remember her?"

He pulled away from her. "No, I don't remember her at all."

Bethani pointed to my shirt. "Angelina, give me your locket."

"Bethani, I…"

"Give it to me!" she demanded, reaching for the collar of my shirt.

I pulled the chain off my neck and handed it to her.

She grabbed it and wrapped it around her hand. She opened the locket and shoved it towards Nicolai's face. "Do you see this couple? This is you and her!"

He studied the picture and shook his head in denial. "I'm sorry, you're mistaken." He looked at me with pleading eyes. "Can I have the key to my room, please?"

Bethani had a wild look in her eyes. "No, you cannot have your room."

Nicolai made a circle motion near his head and rolled his eyes. "This girl's crazy."

"I'll show you crazy!" she screamed, acting out in rage. She grabbed the dagger from my side and thrust it toward Nicolai's heart.

My breath caught in my throat as I jumped in between them. The dagger slid right into my chest and into my heart. He caught me and slid me down to the floor, putting my head in his hands.

* * *

"What have I done?" Bethani fell to the floor and began sobbing.

"No," Daniel whispered.

"What have you done?" Jeremiah glared at Nicolai. "This is your fault!"

Nicolai looked down at the beautiful girl he held in his hands. He stared into her wide chestnut-colored eyes and blinked away part of a memory. "What was that?" he asked, staring deeper.

"You're remembering!" Daniel exclaimed.

Nicolai saw himself holding her once before in the past. Blood pooled around them. He looked up, a huge smile gracing his face. "I remember!" He grabbed the dagger and threw it across the floor.

Jeremiah shook his head in disbelief. "It's too late," he said.

He looked at Jeremiah. "It's never too late when you have something worth fighting for."

Jeremiah studied him and nodded. "Glad to see you back, friend."

"Friend?" Nicolai smirked. "I don't know about that."

"Rude, check," Stephen quipped.

"Still ugly," Nicolai retorted.

Stephen sneered at him. "Still not funny."

Daniel pointed to his sister. "How do we save her?"

"According to the stories my mother told me as a boy, we need to get her back to the portal. Once she crosses through it, death will release the hold it has on her," he answered.

"But she's been stabbed through the heart," Jeremiah said.

"It doesn't matter. She gave her life for me. She faced her regrets and therefore she can move on from it. Death, fortunately for us all, holds no regrets—only those of others."

"Then let's get her out of here!" Daniel urged, pushing them towards the black door.

Nicolai picked up his beloved Angelina and carried her carefully towards the door. She had given up her life for him, and he had given up his life for her. Love truly knew no boundaries.

Chapter 53
Rebirth

The door swung open and they were greeted by Tristan and his father.

"Well, look at what we have here." Tristan laughed. "Give me Angelina."

Nicolai shook his head in disgust. "No."

"I will only ask once more." He looked at Nicolai and demanded, "Give her to me."

Nicolai grit his teeth together. "Don't make me repeat myself."

Bethani walked up to Tristan and smiled. "Your father promised I could come back to save my mother's soul."

Tristan looked past her and at Hades. "I don't really care what my father said."

Bethani looked up at Tristan's father and smiled. "But you care, don't you?"

Hades nodded and glared down at Tristan. "There is a balance that must be maintained, my son. I gave you the coin in hopes that you were mature enough to handle its power."

He pulled the coin out of his pocket. "What are you talking about, father?"

"You saw my agony, and how hard it was for me to come to terms with my mistakes," he answered swiftly. "I thought maybe it had knocked some sense into your head."

"Apparently it didn't." Tristan grimaced, as the coin was ripped out of his hands by Stephen.

"Now you can't use it any longer." The vampire smirked, running down the hallway.

The others followed behind him, carrying Angelina.

"The coin must not leave my side!" Tristan's voice boomed towards them.

Stephen rubbed the coin between his fingers and the portal opened. They fell through it clumsily.

* * *

Hearing the argument, I tried to open my eyes. It felt as if they were glued shut.

"Close it!" I heard Elias say.

I heard something fall next to me in the grass.

"Good job, Stephen!" Elias exclaimed.

A warm hand touched the side of my neck. I assumed they were checking to see if I was dead.

Nicolai's voice quivered. "She's alive!" He pulled my limp body close to him.

"Is she going to be okay?" I heard Bethani ask.

"Yes, she's going to be just fine," Nicolai said.

"Nicolai!" Ctephanyi called out. "Are you okay?!"

"Yes, mother. It's a good day to be alive. My soul is my own, and the dagger is no more."

Laughter erupted all around me. Was I the only one that wasn't finding humor in this situation?

I felt a rugged finger push a strand of my hair away from my face. "What about Tristan?" I heard Daniel say.

"For right now, they're stuck in the Underworld. They can't leave without either of them having a coin."

"Give me that little guy," Stephen said, referring to the coin. "It'll be safer with me than any of you dweebs."

"Man, stop talking about your little guy in front of us," Jeremiah joked.

"That's not what your mom called it," Stephen retorted.

"Can we please not fight for like, one day?" I croaked, finally able to open my eyes.

"She's awake!" Showing a relieved smile, Nicolai helped me sit up.

"Welcome back," Ctephanyi said, smiling.

I was weak, but I used what strength I had to hug Nicolai. "I'm so glad you're okay."

"Once he crossed the portal, his physical body returned to his soul immediately," Ctephanyi answered.

"Like magic," Jeremiah said.

There were happy faces around me. "I have one heck of a headache, that's for sure."

Bethani pushed her hand towards me. "I think this is yours."

Smiling at the sight of my locket, I hugged her and said, "Thank you."

She smiled sheepishly. "The clasp is broken, but we can fix that, and…I'm sorry."

"No, thank you," I said. "You kind of saved me, in a way."

"I did?"

"Of course you did," I said. "You made me believe in something that was worth fighting for."

"Would you look at that?" Elias pointed at the moon. It was returning to its milky white color.

I looked up at Nicolai and sighed. "I made the right choice, didn't I?"

He pushed back my hair and kissed my forehead lovingly. "You saved me."

"No." I put his hand on my stomach. "I saved us."

Chapter 54
Not So Happy Endings

It had been three weeks since I had last visited the Crimson Forest. I couldn't bring myself to return since they had brought me back from the Underworld. Things had quieted down in our small town of Buffalo. Of course, a hazmat team was sent to the area to examine why the deer had acted so insane by running into town. After a short investigation, the deer were returned to the forest.

We had returned to our quaint little bed and breakfast where I spent the first few days in bed recovering from the wound to my chest. It healed quickly but left a small scar. Nicolai spent the next few weeks creating plans for the twins' room while my grandmother decided she was going to stay and help decorate it. Of course, she had to change her appearance so people wouldn't recognize her. I knew she wouldn't be able to stay long, but any time with her was good enough for me.

Bethani rarely left her room. She was still dealing with the fact that she had killed me while in the Underworld. I tried to explain to her a million times that it had to be done, but she just couldn't let it go. Eventually she would come to terms with it At least I hoped so.

Jeremiah and Daniel ended up becoming good buddies and visited often, while Stephen returned to his wily ways of wooing women. Ctephanyi and Elias returned to the forest to rebuild their home for the few of their species that had been found alive. We buried my father and what was left of Mathias next to my mother. I planned to visit them as often as I could manage.

I curled up next to Snow and lay my head across her soft stomach. She was full size now and carried herself with stubborn grace—just like me. Life had finally calmed down and I was beginning to feel normal again. Deep down, I knew that Tristan would find a way to come back, and I would need to be ready for him. It scared me, being pregnant, and having to worry about such things. My family was my world and they were worth fighting for, every step of the way.

Nicolai walked into the room and sat down on the bed next to me. "I love you."

I looked up at him and smiled. "Well, I love you too, sir."

He kissed me tenderly. "You know…you're worth dying for."

Frowning, I gave him a look of disapproval. "That's not funny."

He ran his hands through my hair. "I want this forever, you and I."

I felt my eyes well up with tears. "I want this forever, too."

"You'll always be worth it." He kissed me again, this time more passionately.

I felt a warm tear slide down my cheek. "And you'll always be worth it to me."

He sat back and looked at me in horror. "Angelina, you're bleeding!"

"What?" I reached up and touched my face. I wiped the wetness away from my face and stared at the rusty color on my fingertips. That rusty wetness was blood.

"No," Nicolai whispered. "It can't be."

"What?" I cried out, wiping the blood from my eyes.

He looked down at me, his eyes filling with anger and despair. "They're crimson tears."

Epilogue
Crimson Moon

Tristan's emerald-green eyes glowed with envy. "How could you just let her go that easy?!" he demanded.

His father looked up at him, a blank stare on his stern face. "I do not meddle with things that are bigger than me, and you would be wise not to either."

"Bigger than you?" he cried out, "You're Hades, for Christ's sake!"

He stared at the many souls filtering into the Ocean of the Dead. "I may be Hades, but you, son, have no idea what you're messing with."

"So, you won't help me."

"No, I won't."

"Then I shall do this on my own," he seethed. "You will see just how unstoppable we truly are."

Hades looked back up at him, his dark eyes brooding. "Son."

Tristan ignored him and began to walk away. "I've got no time for anyone who doesn't have time for me."

"Do yourself a favor."

Tristan stopped briefly to hear his father out. "What?" he asked bluntly.

"The crimson tears have fallen."

His heart stopped. "What did you just say?"

"You heard me."

He shook his head in disbelief. "Impossible. How?"

"She crossed back into the land of the living with the pendant."

"That means…"

"She doesn't have much time," his father said.

Tristan's heart began to beat a little faster. He knew what the first crimson tear falling meant. Death.

"You can save her."

"How? I can't even get back without the coin?"

His father turned his eyes away from the empty souls that stared back at him and walked over to his son. "Do you truly care for this human?"

Tristan stared up at his father, pleading in his eyes. "Since the day she was born."

"Why do you love her?"

"What do you mean?"

"It's a simple question, really."

Tristan shoved his hands into the pockets of his pants and felt his face get hot with embarrassment. "I don't know," he replied, rocking back and forth on his heels.

"Then you do not deserve to go back and try to save her," his father said as he began to walk back to the sea of souls.

"Wait."

His father stopped and turned back to face him. "Tell me the truth, son, why do you love this being?"

"Fine," Tristan sighed. "The first time I saw her she had such innocence about her. It was like everything she touched came to life."

A sadness Tristan had never seen washed over his father's face. "She's so much like her mother."

"You loved her mother, didn't you?"

His father gave a little cough, and the stern look returned to his face. "This isn't about me Tristan."

Tristan knew not to say another word about Angelina's mother by the tone of his voice. "Okay, so what do I do? Was my answer good enough for you?"

His father sighed. "Love is such a curious thing. All creatures feel love, did you know that?"

He stared in disbelief at his father's sentiment. "What does that have to do with anything?"

"Well, for you to save her, she must learn to love you. Truly love you."

"Impossible."

His father shook his head. "It is possible."

"How?"

"Love has so many different meanings."

"You're not helping me much with these riddles about love."

His father looked at him, and with a small pat on the back he smiled. "Those riddles, son, are the answer to your question. You must figure them out before it's too late."

"But how do I do that?" he asked, begging his father to tell him.

Hades looked at the dark, swirling Ocean of the Dead before him. "It's time, son."

"Time for what?"

"Time for you to learn about yourself and the one you think you love," he answered, pushing his son into the many souls that crowded the water beside them.

"What are you doing?!" Tristan cried out.

"I've decided to help you, son. Good luck."

Tristan felt the life being sucked out of his body. He couldn't breathe and gasped for air. How could his father betray him like this? How could he throw him into the Ocean of the Dead and let him wither away into nothing?

The darkness clouded his thoughts and he could feel his soul slowly starting to slip away. He thrust his hand into the air and hoped his father would reach in and pull him out, but the darkness took hold of him and he closed his eyes. His time had come—or had it?

Suddenly he opened his eyes and gasped for air. He looked around and saw he had washed up on the bank of the river that skirted the village of Buffalo.

He rolled over and spit out the water that had settled in his lungs. He wiped the water from his eyes and noticed something strange. He looked down at his hands. His usual pale skin tone had changed to a dark olive color.

"What the...?" he questioned.

He stood up and noticed he his body shape was also different. "He changed my appearance!" he said out loud, a frown on his face. For a moment, he couldn't understand why his father would do such a thing to him and then, slowly, a smile began to form on his new face. "This is perfect. She'll never see me coming." He laughed and silently thanked his father.

Now he would make Angelina his. He would make her fall in love with him and save her before the last crimson tear fell from her beautiful chestnut-colored eyes.

The End

Acknowledgements

JD—I want to thank you as you were my strength throughout this entire process and I will never be able to thank you enough for everything. I love you, husband! F Trees Baby!

Zara & Allan—You are my family. You've believed in me since the beginning and have taken me in like I am one of your own. I will forever be eternally grateful for everything you've done for me.

Matt Kramer—My brother from my surrogate mother! You always have that hug when I need it and know just what to say to make me smile. You are one of the most amazing people I have ever met, and I want to thank you for well…everything.

Tom Suder—Bossman, I still haven't quit and have no intentions on quitting. Now read this book series!

Andrew—My #1 biggest fan in the whole entire world! When I saw the excitement in your eyes after you read *Crimson Forest*, it let me know that this was indeed the path that was created for me to follow. Thank you!

Arlette & Sarah—You have both taken me in as a sister and part of your family. I am so incredibly honored to be considered as such. I love you both very much and thank you for allowing me to be a part of something so loving and so amazing.

Claudette & John—You welcomed me and my children into your amazing family and have treated us with dignity and shown us nothing but love and respect. I want to thank you for allowing my children and me to be a part of such an amazing family. You should be very proud of yourselves for raising such admirable children. It's something that we will cherish in our hearts forever.

Stephanie Gerold, Christopher Bolen, Missy Fowler, Daniel Harvey, Elyse Ross, and Kim Amburgey—I f'n' love you guys. You guys always listen to me when I have a rough day and have pushed me every step of the way to become the person I was meant to become. I hold each one of you close to my heart and will forever.

And finally, I want to thank all my fans around the world for making *Crimson Forest* such an incredible success. I hope you love *Crimson Moon* just as much and can't wait to release *Crimson Tears*. You are all so amazing and I love each and every single one of you!

P.S. Send me an email at Christine.Gabriel@PandamoonPublishing.com and one lucky person will get to be a character in my next book series! Good luck!

About the Author

Christine Gabriel is a caffeine-fueled dream weaver who lives in the Lake Erie harbor town of Vermilion, Ohio, with her husband JD, four children, and two furbabies. Blessed with an overactive imagination, she enjoys creating fictional characters and worlds that make you question where the line between fantasy and reality exists. Christine adores interacting with her fans in real life and on social media. Seeing her readers smile is what motivates her to continue sharing her creative stories with the world.

Thank you for reading this copy of *Crimson Moon,* **Book 2 in** *The Crimson Chronicles.* If you enjoyed this book, please let the author know by posting a review.

Growing good ideas into great reads…one book at a time.

Visit www.pandamoonpublishing.com to learn more about other works by our talented authors.

Mystery/Thriller/Suspense

- *A Flash of Red* by Sarah K. Stephens
- *Evening in the Yellow Wood* by Laura Kemp
- *Fate's Past* by Jason Huebinger
- *Graffiti Creek* by Matt Coleman
- *Juggling Kittens* by Matt Coleman
- *Killer Secrets* by Sherrie Orvik
- *Knights of the Shield* by Jeff Messick
- *Kricket* by Penni Jones
- *Looking into the Sun* by Todd Tavolazzi
- *On the Bricks Series Book 1: On the Bricks* by Penni Jones
- *Rogue Saga Series Book 1: Rogue Alliance* by Michelle Bellon
- *Southbound* by Jason Beem
- *The Juliet* by Laura Ellen Scott
- *The Last Detective* by Brian Cohn
- *The Moses Winter Mysteries Book 1: Made Safe* by Francis Sparks
- *The New Royal Mysteries Book 1: The Mean Bone in Her Body* by Laura Ellen Scott
- *The New Royal Mysteries Book 2: Crybaby Lane* by Laura Ellen Scott
- *The Ramadan Drummer* by Randolph Splitter
- *The Teratologist* by Ward Parker
- *The Unraveling of Brendan Meeks* by Brian Cohn
- *The Zeke Adams Series Book 1: Pariah* by Ward Parker
- *This Darkness Got to Give* by Dave Housley

Science Fiction/Fantasy

- *Becoming Thuperman* by Elgon Williams
- *Children of Colondona Book 1: The Wizard's Apprentice* by Alisse Lee Goldenberg
- *Children of Colondona Book 2: The Island of Mystics* by Alisse Lee Goldenberg
- *Chimera Catalyst* by Susan Kuchinskas
- *Dybbuk Scrolls Trilogy Book 1: The Song of Hadariah* by Alisse Lee Goldenberg
- *Dybbuk Scrolls Trilogy Book 2: The Song of Vengeance* by Alisse Lee Goldenberg
- *Dybbuk Scrolls Trilogy Book 3: The Song of War* by Alisse Lee Goldenberg
- *Everly Series Book 1: Everly* by Meg Bonney
- *.EXE Chronicles Book 1: Hello World* by Alexandra Tauber and Tiffany Rose
- *Fried Windows (In a Light White Sauce)* by Elgon Williams
- *Magehunter Saga Book 1: Magehunter* by Jeff Messick
- *Project 137* by Seth Augenstein
- *Revengers Series Book 1: Revengers* by David Valdes Greenwood
- *The Bath Salts Journals: Volume One* by Alisse Lee Goldenberg and An Tran
- *The Crimson Chronicles Book 1: Crimson Forest* by Christine Gabriel
- *The Crimson Chronicles Book 2: Crimson Moon* by Christine Gabriel
- *The Phaethon Series Book 1: Phaethon* by Rachel Sharp
- *The Sitnalta Series Book 1: Sitnalta* by Alisse Lee Goldenberg
- *The Sitnalta Series Book 2: The Kingdom Thief* by Alisse Lee Goldenberg
- *The Sitnalta Series Book 3: The City of Arches* by Alisse Lee Goldenberg
- *The Sitnalta Series Book 4: The Hedgewitch's Charm* by Alisse Lee Goldenberg
- *The Sitnalta Series Book 5: The False Princess* by Alisse Lee Goldenberg
- *The Wolfcat Chronicles Book 1: Wolfcat 1* by Elgon Williams

Women's Fiction

- *Beautiful Secret* by Dana Faletti
- *The Long Way Home* by Regina West
- *The Mason Siblings Series Book 1: Love's Misadventure* by Cheri Champagne
- *The Mason Siblings Series Book 2: The Trouble with Love* by Cheri Champagne
- *The Mason Siblings Series Book 3: Love and Deceit* by Cheri Champagne
- *The Mason Siblings Series Book 4: Final Battle for Love* by Cheri Champagne
- *The Seductive Spies Series Book 1: The Thespian Spy* by Cheri Champagne
- *The Seductive Spy Series Book 2: The Seamstress and the Spy* by Cheri Champagne
- *The Shape of the Atmosphere* by Jessica Dainty
- *The To-Hell-And-Back Club Book 1: The To-Hell-And-Back Club* by Jill Hannah Anderson
- *The To-Hell-And-Back Club Book 2: Crazy Little Town Called Love* by Jill Hannah Anderson

CPSIA information can be obtained
at www.ICGtesting.com
Printed in the USA
BVHW061652080419
544915BV00017B/1590/P